"Will you tell him of your...escapade?"

Mitch's words thrust the knife-edge of guilt deeper, and she turned on him, hating him. "What makes you think I won't?" Ashleigh retorted angrily. "Jonathan is a fair-minded adult. He's kind and he's understanding and he—" she gulped a breath "—he happens to love me."

"Love has a habit of turning a levelheaded adult into an evil-tempered, narrow-minded juvenile," Mitch said with his cynical smile in place.

"And you are obviously judging everyone by your own predictable reactions!" Ashleigh threw back at him. "Jonathan will understand the situation, the circumstances."

His laugh was harsh. "He's either a namby-pamby or some sort of god. At least you'd get an honest reaction out of me—out of any normal man whose fiancée has made love to another man."

Tropical Knight

by

LYNSEY STEVENS

Harlequin Books

TORONTO • NEW YORK • LOS ANGELES • LONDON
AMSTERDAM • PARIS • SYDNEY • HAMBURG
STOCKHOLM • ATHENS • TOKYO • MILAN

Original hardcover edition published in 1982
by Mills & Boon Limited

ISBN 0-373-02507-6

Harlequin Romance first edition October 1982

CHAPTER ONE

THE plane seemed to dip alarmingly and Ashleigh gripped the arms of her seat and closed her eyes, swallowing to relieve the pressure in her ears. How she hated flying! It crossed her mind, as it had quite often in the past few days, that there was something to be said for being an orphan. A reluctant smile lifted the corners of her mouth as she recalled the wounded look on her mother's face when she had said as much just before her flight number was called.

The family was aware of how much she disliked flying, but that hadn't stopped them all deciding she was to be the one to be despatched on this errand of mercy to save Gemma from what their mother seemed to put on a par with a fate worse than death. Poor Gemma! She'd really thrown Mother into a tailspin. Ashleigh grimaced at her choice of expression. Tailspin wasn't the type of word she wanted to couple with aeroplane just at the moment. She forced her thoughts along different channels.

She supposed she should sympathise with her mother, who considered herself to have a large cross to bear in the unenviable task of marrying off a tribe of seven daughters. When Ashleigh married in a month's time her mother would have passed the halfway mark, with four down and three to go. Ashleigh suppressed a chuckle at her thoughts.

Not that she didn't admire her mother, and her father for that matter. Raising a family of seven girls was no mean feat and Ashleigh considered they had

5

been raised very well. However, it was her mother and four of her sisters that Ashleigh had had to face when she arrived home on Friday afternoon.

She remembered the immense feeling of pleasure that came over her as she turned her Mini into the tree-lined avenue of Lavender Street and drove down to the end where the rambling old Colonial house that had housed the Craigs through a couple of generations stood among the huge spreading poinciana and mango trees. It was an ecstatic feeling to know that you had finished work for six whole weeks and that in four weeks you would be marrying a very nice considerate man and would be living happily ever after.

The double gates lay permanently open, and as Ashleigh turned between the large white gateposts she noticed that the brass plaque on one post saying William Craig, M.D. needed polishing again. And as she crawled easily up the drive she had a feeling that all was right with her world.

Recalling those feelings, Ashleigh almost gave a cynical laugh. She should have known that something was in the wind when she saw her twelve-year-old sister Debbie, the baby of the family, playing with the children. Judging by the number it was the complete set of her nephews and nieces. For them all to be visiting on a Friday afternoon, en masse, should have prepared her, but she felt no premonition as they all clustered round the car to hug and kiss Aunty Ash.

'Hi, Deb!' Ashleigh smiled at her sister, kicking the children's soccer ball and watching them chase after it. 'Mmm, it feels great to know I haven't got to face those enquiring little minds for six whole weeks!'

'That's hardly the right attitude, Ash,' remarked

Debbie grandly. 'I thought you teachers liked to mould young minds.'

'Don't you believe it! Some of those engaging little souls can out-mould ten adults,' Ashleigh laughed. She loved her job and wouldn't have changed it for anything. 'Anyway, six weeks of bliss ahead.'

'That's exactly how I see the hols. No more ghastly maths!' Debbie pulled a face.

'Come on, Deb,' called Melissa, 'the boys are winning. We need you.'

'Okay!' she called. 'See you, Ash.' Debbie went to run off and then stopped, turning a teasing smile on her sister. 'Good luck inside!'

'Good luck for what?' Ashleigh smiled back, unsuspecting.

'You'll see,' Debbie laughed, and dashed for the ball her niece kicked towards her.

Ashleigh ran up the wide front steps and crossed the verandah. A babble of voices tumbled from the living-room off the hall to Ashleigh's left. Dropping her briefcase thankfully on the telephone table, she walked into the room, to be met with what seemed like a sea of familiar faces, all crying welcomes. Her mother sat in the middle, her sprained ankle propped on a footstool.

'Ashleigh dear—you're late,' she smiled faintly. 'We were about to send off a search party.'

'The teachers at work threw me a little party after break-up,' Ashleigh explained. 'You should see the lovely dinner set they gave me. Oh, dear, I've left it in the car. I was terrified it would get broken, so I put it on the floor in the back seat. I'll just pop out and get it.' She went to leave the room, but her mother waved her hand.

'In a minute, dear. We want to talk to you.'

Ashleigh then noticed the frown of concern on her

mother's face and that the hand she waved clutched a letter.

'What's the trouble, Mother?' She sat down on the arm of her father's large stuffed chair. 'With everyone here it looks like a Round Table conference!'

Her four sisters laughed, but her mother continued to frown.

'This is serious, girls.' Her mother fluttered the letter in Ashleigh's direction. 'It's Gemma.'

'Gemma?' Ashleigh sobered. 'What's wrong with Gem? She isn't sick, is she?'

'Would it were that simple!' Her mother rolled her eyes and paused for effect. 'She's engaged,' she said as though she was delivering news of a major disaster.

'Engaged? Gemma?' Ashleigh was surprised, to say the least. Of all her sisters twenty-year-old Gemma was the quietest, always lost in amongst the more outgoing personalities of the rest of the family. And when it came to men Gemma was almost painfully shy.

Six months earlier she had been sent up to Central Queensland on transfer with her position in the bank. She was to instruct the staff in the bank's branch at Airlie Beach in the use of a new ledger machine that had been installed. It was only the sudden illness of one member of the bank's staff that had extended her stay up there.

'Are you sure she said engaged?' Ashleigh asked.

Mrs Craig's expression was wounded. 'How could I mistake that, Ashleigh?' She shook her head. 'Oh, dear, I'm nearly sick with worry! For Gemma to write such news at this particular moment is such a frustration for me. Here I am with this wretched foot and your father away for the week at his conference in Sydney. Otherwise I tell you I'd have been on the very first plane heading up there to see what was going on. I mean,' she appealed to her eldest daughter, 'if it was any of the others . . . But Gemma. Who's to say who this young man may be? He could be anyone!'

'What does Gemma say exactly?' Ashleigh asked, and everyone began talking at once.

'He sounds like a hunk to me,' remarked eighteen-year-old Louise, 'even if he is a bit old on it. Thirty or something, wasn't he?'

'She can't have known him very long,' put in Nina. 'Mum says she's never mentioned him in any of her other letters.'

'Maybe we shouldn't prejudge him,' said Vicki, moving herself into a more comfortable position in her chair. 'He might be quite nice.'

'Yes, Mum. I can't see Gem wanting to marry someone unsuitable,' added Adrie, saving her ear-ring from the chubby fingers of her baby son.

'She says he's quite rich,' said her mother accusingly.

'Great!' said Louise. 'Handsome and rich—what more could you want, Mum? He can't be all bad.'

'Gemma says they want to get married quietly in a couple of months. Oh, Ashleigh, this is terrible! I feel almost ill over it. My daughter needs me and I'm tied here like a helpless cripple.'

'Mother, what could you do if you did go up there? Gemma would still want to marry him,' said Ashleigh. 'What else did she say about him? What's he do for a living?'

Mrs Craig lifted her glasses from their resting place on her ample bosom, suspended around her neck on a gold chain, and popped them on her nose. 'Let's see.' She unfolded the letter, scanned the first page and turned to the second. 'She says, "He's one of the nicest, kindest people I've ever met. His family own boats that take tourists out to the Whitsunday Islands."' Mrs Craig almost shuddered. ' "And Joel", that's his name, "manages the whole operation."'

'Read Ash the part about his brother, Mum,' broke in Louise.

'Oh. Oh, yes. Here it is. "Joel's brother Ryan, and his wife Liv, who's really nice, own a fantastic resort on one of the islands. You may have heard of it— Craven Island. It's quite well known."'

'I've heard about it,' said Louise. 'It's supposed to be *the* island resort. I don't know why you're so worried, Mum. They sound loaded. Do you think they'll let us have a free holiday on the island?'

'Business is business, you mercenary creature,' remarked Adrie.

'I don't care about money where my daughters are concerned,' said Mrs Craig. 'All I ask is that they be happy and their husbands are nice and kind.'

'Gemma says he's nice and kind,' Vicki reminded her.

Mrs Craig looked unconvinced.

'Well, I don't know, Mother,' Ashleigh shrugged. 'Gem's twenty, she's hardly a baby. And she's level-headed. I'm sure she knows what she's doing.'

'Ashleigh, how can you say that? How can you be so uncaring? For all we know, this . . . this Joel Denison, or whatever he chooses to call himself, may be taking advantage of a young girl who's away from home for the first time. Gemma's terribly naïve about the ways of the world.'

'If he's rich he can't be after her money,' began Vicki.

'Mum's talking about him being after Gem's body,' laughed Louise. 'Quit worrying, Mum. She knows all about the birds and bees—I told her before she left.'

'Louise!' admonished her mother.

Ashleigh laughed at her sister and then sobered at her mother's stern expression. 'Maybe you could phone her at work and talk to her,' she suggested feebly.

Mrs Craig shook her head. 'No. The only thing that will put my mind at rest would be to see just what this young man is like first-hand.'

'Mother, you can't go up there with your sprained ankle—Dad would have a fit!'

'I know I can't go,' said her mother with a sigh. 'But you can, Ashleigh.'

'Me? Oh, now wait a minute, Mother.' Ashleigh stood up. 'I've got too much to do with the wedding in four weeks' time. It's right out of the question.'

'Ashleigh dear, I'd go myself if I thought I could hobble through,' Mrs Craig sighed deeply again, 'but I can't,' she finished quietly.

Ashleigh felt the pang of guilt she was meant to feel and glanced around at her sisters for support.

'You're the only one who's free to go,' continued her mother. 'Nina and Rex and the children have made arrangements to spend the next three weeks with Rex's parents. Adrie can't go with the baby and with Vicki due to have her baby any time—well, it would be impossible.'

'I said I'd go, Mum,' put in Louise cheerfully.

'Yes, and then we'd have to despatch someone to see what you were getting up to,' replied her mother, and turned imploring eyes on her eldest daughter. 'You see, dear, there's only you.'

'Mother,' Ashleigh appealed to her again, 'you know my dress isn't even started nor are the bridesmaids' outfits. There's all the arrangements to double check. I can't go flitting about the countryside!'

'It would only take a couple of days, Ashleigh,' said her mother. 'If you left on Monday morning you could probably be back by Wednesday. You can have a fitting for your dress before you go and it can be ready to try on when you come back.'

'Mother, have a heart! Even if I could get a seat up there at the beginning of the holiday season you know how I detest flying,' Ashleigh finished lamely.

Mrs Craig triumphantly held up another envelope. 'There was a last-minute cancellation on Monday's flight. I've sent Gemma a telegram to say you're coming and to meet you at the airport.' Her mother smiled innocently.

'Oh, Mother!' Ashleigh shook her head in exasperation. 'You have fists of iron beneath those kid gloves.'

'Don't despair, Ash,' teased Louise. 'Maybe there's another brother who'll sweep you off your feet.'

'I'd hardly be interested if he had half a dozen brothers,' said Ashleigh drily.

'Pity,' remarked Louise. 'I guess you'll just have to settle for Jonathan, then.'

'I'm not "settling" for Jonathan,' said Ashleigh, feeling a spurt of anger. 'I happen to be in love with him.'

'But, Ash, he's so unlike you. He's staid—and old.'

'Thirty-eight is not old,' defended Ashleigh.

'Stop hassling Ashleigh, Louise,' Adrie came to her sister's aid. 'Jonathan's all right.'

Ashleigh took a quick look through her window at the distant tableau that was the coastal strip below and her hands gripped together. Fortunately they would be there in less than fifteen minutes if they were running to schedule. In Mackay they had changed planes for the second leg of the trip, and the smaller aircraft only served to increase Ashleigh's trepidation.

'Jonathan's all right!' Her sister's words returned to her and she frowned faintly. Was that how everyone saw him? She brought his face into her mind. He really was quite good-looking, distinguished. In fact he looked exactly what he was, a successful accountant.

They'd known each other for seven years, had been engaged for over eighteen months and were completely at one each with the other. Didn't they have so much in common, enjoy the same things? Music. Books. Sport. At squash they were well matched, with Jonathan just having the edge on her. And they wanted the same things out of life.

After they were married they would be moving into the house Jonathan owned and Ashleigh would continue teaching for a while. In a year or so they would be starting a family; they'd decided on two children fairly close together. It was all so simple.

Ashleigh shifted uneasily in the confines of her narrow seat as the word 'boring' crossed her mind. What was the matter with her? Wasn't it all just the way she wanted it? Jonathan wasn't the type to throw discretion to the wind, sweep her off her feet. He gave any decision considerable thought and always decided on what was for the best in the long run. That was sensible. And staid. Wasn't that how Louise had described it?

No, Jonathan wasn't staid. He was merely . . . merely sensible. There was a difference. And how many times has he kissed you as though he didn't want to stop at kisses? asked a tiny voice somewhere in the back of her mind. Ashleigh's frown deepened. Jonathan respected her. And besides, she was past all that mad youthful passion. She was now a sensible twenty-eight-year-old and she had got that sort of relationship out of her system when she was young and foolish.

Foolish and young—those words often went hand in hand, and she couldn't deny she had been both young and foolish. And it was only the fact that fate had stepped in so cruelly that had kept her from taking a giant step into trouble.

Her heart constricted painfully as her thoughts flew back to those few mad months at the beginning of her course at training college, months filled with the joy and agony, the intensity of a first real love. Could it possibly have been her, lost in that youthful need?

Strange, she hadn't thought about him in ages, and after all these years—could it be ten years?—she could still see his face, feel the sadness of his loss. Poor Robbie, so tall and broad and full of life. Long fair hair and dancing eyes, nose slightly bent, a legacy of a Rugby League match. How she had adored him! He was popular with everyone, always had everyone laughing, joking, feeling good. And he'd wanted just ordinary Ashleigh Craig.

A tiny feeling, long dormant, stirred within her. He wanted her to spend the weekend with him and he'd arranged the loan of a flat down at the coast. Another couple were going along, but Ashleigh knew what he was asking and she had accepted, if somewhat guiltily. She loved him and that was all that mattered. On his way to collect her for the weekend his car had gone out of control on a patch of oil on the road and a young life had been so tragically wasted.

Time could not totally erode the remembered pain of his loss, and it had taken Ashleigh literally years to come to terms with his death and with herself. Meeting Jonathan had been the beginning, so she was grateful to him for that. That uncomfortable feeling crept over her again. Gratitude? You couldn't build a solid marriage on . . .!

For heaven's sake, she admonished herself. What had happened to the girl who had smugly driven home on Friday afternoon with a happy and contented heart? It was the upset of this trip, she told herself, wishing she had simply refused to come. But of course, one couldn't refuse Mother anything.

The sign flashed to fasten seat-belts and Ashleigh's heart thumped loudly in her ears as the plane began its descent. Only when the wheels bumped on to the runway did she let out the breath she was holding. It was irrational to have this fear of flying, but try as she might she had been unable to overcome it, and she doubted she ever would.

Inside the small terminal she looked around expectantly for her sister, but there was no sign of Gemma anywhere. After a few minutes Ashleigh went to collect her small suitcase and returned to the main area, but Gemma had still not arrived.

Frowning, Ashleigh checked her watch. Oh well, Gem was only ten minutes late; perhaps she was held up at work. She strolled across to a vacant seat and sat down to wait. The air was humid and her head still ached from the plane trip. She could feel the white material of her simply cut summer dress beginning to cling to her back and she ran her fingers through the dampness beneath her short fair hair.

Where was Gemma? Surely she'd received Mother's

telegram. Twenty minutes later Ashleigh was beginning to feel alarmed. Perhaps she should check to see if Gemma had left a message for her at the enquiries counter. But they would have paged her in that case. Well, there was always a taxi, she told herself. She'd give her until the half hour.

A few minutes later a tall broad-shouldered figure strode purposefully into the waiting area, dragged sunglasses from his nose, pausing hands on hips to glance about the room. Ashleigh froze, her breath caught in her throat. In that first moment she had thought he was Robbie and she knew her face paled. He had that same thick fair hair, bleached almost white from the sun, and he carried himself in the same upright manner. But Robbie was dead!

The man's gaze moved about the room and after he had ascertained that Ashleigh was the only person waiting he began to stride across to her. As he approached her she could see that he was really nothing like Robbie as far as facial features went. Robbie had always been smiling, but there was no humour in this man's craggy face. She was being fanciful. Robbie had been on her mind and it was easy for her to conjure him out of a vague resemblance. Her eyes remembered to move from his face, quickly took in the rest of him, wishing she had the self-possession to allow her eyes to slide over him in the familiar way his eyes were boldly examining her, and her lips tightened. How she hated men who did that! It was so rude.

He looked as though he had come straight from hours of manual labour, from the tips of his dark blue sneaker-clad feet to the windswept disorder of his longish hair. His blue stubby shorts and pale blue T-shirt moulded his large frame, and reluctantly Ashleigh found her eyes drawn to the muscular strength of him. His legs were long and tanned and muscular and he was obviously very fit.

He approached with a firm unhurried tread, unabashed by her appraisal, and stopped in front of her, hands again on hips and eyes narrowed as he looked unsmilingly down at her.

'Miss Ashleigh Craig?' His voice was deep and blatantly masculine and Ashleigh felt a stirring of irrational irritation. Perhaps because seated, he had her at a disadvantage, standing towering over her.

'Yes?' Her own voice was sharp, her face set to freeze him off.

A cynical smile lifted the corners of his mouth and his eyes roved over her again with thorough insolence. 'Gemma sent me to collect you.'

'Why didn't Gemma come herself?' Ashleigh stood up, drawing herself up to her full five foot six inches. She still had to lift her head to look at him and a frown touched her brow.

'She was on her way, but it seems she had a slight accident in her car,' he told her without preamble.

'An accident? What happened? Is she all right?'

'As far as I know,' he said. 'But I haven't got any of the details.'

'As far as you know?' Ashleigh's temper rose. 'And as far as you care, too, by the sound of it!' she blazed at him, her worry over her sister adding a bite to her voice.

'She assured me she was only shaken up,' he shrugged, 'but the car was out of action, so here I am.'

'I don't know you from Adam.' Ashleigh raised her chin. 'I'll get a taxi, thank you.' She picked up her case and went to step past him.

'Now listen, lady.' Strong brown fingers snaked around her arm, burning where they touched. 'If I have to leave off my work to come pick up a sister of Gemma's then by God I'll pick her up.'

'Take your hands off me!' Ashleigh bit out, her blue eyes dark, raking him.

He took no notice of her command, still held her arm firmly, and he shook his head slightly. 'Are you sure you're Gemma's sister?'

'Of course I am,' she replied angrily. 'But exactly how you come to know my sister you've failed to explain. My God!' A thought crossed her mind with shocking suddenness. 'You can't be . . . you're not Joel Denison, are you?'

'Sorry to disappoint you.' His smile was mocking. 'Not likely, wouldn't you say? Gem wouldn't touch me with a ten-foot pole. I'd scare her to death if I looked sideways at her. Your sister's a very nice little mouse, Ashleigh Craig.' His smile widened. 'It doesn't appear to run in the family.'

'Gemma is not a mouse. She's simply a shy, considerate person,' Ashleigh retorted. 'And you still haven't answered my question. Who are you?'

'Oh, just call me one of the poor relations.' He smiled crookedly again. 'Mitchell Patrick—Mitch if you want to be friendly. I'm Joel's cousin.'

'Well, Mr Patrick, for a start you can let me go before I kick you in your very vulnerable shins. Then I can find a taxi to take me to Gemma's. She may be in hospital for all the interest you seem to have shown.'

'Look, your sister is at home. She rang me from the flat next door and asked me to collect you so that you wouldn't have to resort to a taxi, so the sooner I deliver you to her flat the sooner I can get back to work. My Range Rover's outside, so how about it?'

Ashleigh looked pointedly down at his hand on her arm and he slowly released her. 'Thank you,' she said with an edge of sarcasm. 'I suppose Gemma would be upset if I arrived in a taxi,' she frowned and turned to him. 'As you say, the sooner we leave the sooner you can return to work. And the sooner I can reassure myself about Gemma.'

'At your service, Miss Craig.' He gave a slight bow before taking her case from her fingers and leading the way out into the fierce sunshine. He opened the passenger side door with almost exaggerated politeness and Ashleigh, sensing he was laughing at her, gritted her teeth and climbed up into the four-wheel-drive. It was in good condition, she noticed, and bore the insignia of D. J. Denison and Company on the door.

Mitch Patrick returned his sunglasses to his nose as he strode purposefully around the front of the car. Fishing around in her handbag, Ashleigh found her own dark glasses and thankfully slipped them on.

'Is it far to Gemma's flat?' she asked in what she hoped was a relaxed conversational tone.

'Not so far,' he replied, shifting gears smoothly, his hand strong and tanned. 'Tell me, Miss Craig, what do you hope to gain from this flying visit? Hoping to talk your sister out of it?'

Ashleigh turned to him in surprise. 'What do you mean by that?'

He shot her a quick look. 'Oh, come now, Miss Craig. I know Gemma told her family about her engagement last week, in fact, I posted the letter for her, and now here you are. Simple.'

'I don't care what you think you know, Mr Patrick,'

Ashleigh replied with more outward calm than she felt. 'I'm here to see Gemma. Surely that's not too difficult to credit?'

He laughed shortly. 'You didn't come before. Gem gets engaged and post-haste her maiden sister hares up to save the day.'

'I am not a maiden sister!' Ashleigh began, seething at his insolence.

He looked at her again, one fine eyebrow raised, and she could feel his eyes behind his sunglasses as they moved over her again. 'You're not? Interesting!' he said suggestively.

Ashleigh's lips thinned. 'You are vulgar and ill-bred, Mr Patrick,' she said with anger. 'Someone like you couldn't possibly understand that Gemma is part of a loving family. We care about her and we care what happens to her. I've come to meet her fiancé on behalf of our family. So take that any way you like to, I really couldn't care less.' She looked steadily out of the side window, not taking in the greenery of her surroundings, the palms, the colourful hibiscus shrubs.

'You're pretty good at putting people in their place,' he said at last. 'You tell it like it is.' He chuckled, a deep vibration in his chest that set Ashleigh's nerve ends jangling. 'You know, I think I could get to like you, Ashleigh.'

'Don't put yourself under any strain on my account,' she remarked through clenched teeth as he swung the Range Rover into the parking area of a single-storey block of flats and switched off the engine. Turning to her again, he shook his head. 'You and Gem are complete opposites—in temperament, I mean. Pity you didn't have another sister who was a happy medium—your fire and Gem's tranquillity.'

'We have five other sisters, Mr Patrick, and apart from not wishing you on any of them I doubt we could meet your exactingly meticulous standards.' Her eyes, complementing her words, moved derrogatorily over him before she reached for the door handle.

'I'm beginning to think you just might come close, Ashleigh.' His voice was sensuously low and his eyes fell appreciatively over the angry rise and fall of her full breasts down to the slim leg showing where her skirt had ridden up. 'Should be fun putting it to the test.'

'Sorry to be the one to bring bad tidings, but sadly you won't get the chance to test anything.' She held up her left hand to display her engagement ring. 'I'm getting married in exactly three weeks and four days' time.' She smiled with mock ruefulness. 'Looks like you dip out again.' And thoroughly enjoying the knowledge that she had had the last word, Ashleigh opened the door and climbed down on to the asphalt as Gemma, her knee bandaged, came hobbling across the grass.

'Ash—Ash! Hi!' Gemma's arms went around her sister. 'Gee, it's good to see you!' she cried excitedly.

'You, too, love.' Ashleigh smiled. 'Are you okay?'

'Fine. A bit shaken up and a cut on my knee,' Gemma grimaced, and turned shyly to the man who turned from the Range Rover with Ashleigh's case. 'Thanks for collecting Ashleigh for me, Mitch. With Joel over on the island you were the only person I could think of to help out. I hope I didn't drag you away from anything important.'

The smile Mitch Patrick turned on Gemma completely changed his rugged face, and Ashleigh blinked at the transformation and for some reason her heart flipped over alarmingly. He touched Gemma's cheek with one finger and she blushed. 'No trouble, Gem. Joel would have had my hide if I didn't look out for you.'

'Would you like to come in for coffee?' Gemma asked.

'No, thanks. Another time. I have to get back to work.' His smile was cynical again as he turned to Ashleigh. 'Nice meeting you, Miss Craig.'

'Thank you for the lift.' Ashleigh tried to sound gracious.

'Any time,' he replied.

'We'll see you, Mitch,' put in Gemma.

'That you will.' His eyes went back to Ashleigh and he smiled crookedly again. 'You surely will,' he repeated quietly, climbed into the four-wheel-drive and reversed out of the park.

CHAPTER TWO

'OH, Ashleigh, it's really great to see one of the family again,' smiled Gemma as she settled herself back on her chair and arranged a cushion under her bandaged knee. 'I miss everyone so much.'

'We've missed you, too, Gem. Who else can act as the mediator in all our arguments?' asked Ashleigh, trying to swallow her ill-humour and put the infuriating Mitch Patrick out of her mind. 'But tell me, what happened to you?'

'Oh. It was only a minor accident,' said Gemma, 'but the mudguard of my car was pushed on to the tyre so I couldn't drive it. I've left it at the panel beating shop to be fixed.' She sighed. 'And I so wanted to drive you around the area! I even took a couple of days off work,' she added ruefully.

'As long as you're all right,' said Ashleigh.

'It's only a small cut, a bruise mainly,' Gemma shrugged. 'I caught it on the window winder, I think. Just when we could have had a great few days!'

'Not to worry. We can have a good old gossip.'

Gemma laughed softly and then sobered. 'Oh, Ash, I hope Mother wasn't too upset when she received my letter—about Joel, I mean.' A slow blush touched her cheeks, making her look very young and pretty.

Ashleigh grimaced. 'I suppose you've guessed that's the reason why I'm here?'

'I thought as much,' Gemma nodded, and sighed softly. 'I'm really sorry to be the cause of upsetting all your plans, Ash. You must be right in the middle of the wedding arrangements. Did Jonathan mind you coming up here?'

Ashleigh shrugged and passed over the last question. 'What's a couple of days here or there? Now, tell me all. What's Joel like?'

'Oh, Ash, he's wonderful!' Gemma's face glowed, and a tiny pain encircled her sister's heart.

Had she ever felt about Jonathan the way Gemma looked just talking about Joel?

'I know that sounds biased,' Gemma was saying, 'but, Ash, you'll love him, too. And I know when they meet him that Mum and Dad will understand why he's the one for me. He's so . . . so nice.' She laughed a little selfconsciously.

'How did you come to meet him?'

'I met him at the bank, of all places, just after I arrived up here. But I didn't say anything to Mum and Dad because . . . oh, well, I just wanted to keep it to myself for a while. You know?' she appealed to her sister, and Ashleigh nodded, smiling.

'His family do all their business through our branch of the bank and Joel came to see the manager, Mr Donovan. Well, I nearly cannoned into Joel in the hallway. I was so embarrassed, Ash. I tried to apologise—and then he smiled at me.' She shook her head. 'My legs went weak and I just clammed up and went bright red. He's so handsome, tall and dark, with blue eyes, and the nicest smile you could imagine.'

'He sounds like a movie star,' laughed Ashleigh, wondering why she should only be able to recall Jonathan's scowling expression at this particular moment.

'He could easily be one if he wanted to,' replied

Gemma seriously. 'After that day in the bank I didn't even dare to hope I'd see him again, but we accidentally met down at the village the very next day. He . . . he asked me to have lunch with him and we talked practically the whole afternoon. He's so easy to talk to, Ash. I didn't even realise I was talking so much until we went to leave.' Gemma smiled happily. 'We've been going out together ever since and . . . and last week he took me out to a special dinner and he . . . he asked me to marry him. And I said yes.'

Ashleigh smiled. 'You do sound rather smitten.'

'I am. I just can't believe he feels the same way about me. I mean, I've always been the plain Jane of the family. I'm not beautiful or bubbling with personality like you are, Ash.'

'What's all this not beautiful talk?' broke in Ashleigh. 'You're a very attractive girl, Gem, and obviously your Joel knows it.'

And her young sister, so apparently in love, was beautiful. Her young face glowed.

'It's nice of you to say so, Ashleigh. I guess . . . well, I suppose I don't have much self-confidence,' she sighed. 'It's all like a wonderful, wonderful dream. Joel's so . . . Oh, Ash, I can't wait for you to meet him!' Gemma exclaimed.

'And when can I meet him?' asked her sister. 'You know I've been deputised on behalf of the family to look him over,' she teased with mock seriousness. 'So don't be at all surprised if I ask him about his health,' she marked the points off on her fingers, 'quiz him about his prospects, and his intentions, not forgetting to check his teeth.'

Gemma laughed delightedly. 'I think you and Joel will get on marvellously, Ash. He'll be coming back from Craven Island this afternoon and he's coming to dinner tonight. I spoke to him on the phone just before you arrived and when he heard about my accident he decided he'd bring our meal with him so I won't have to do any cooking.' She smiled again. 'He really cares about me, Ash. So you can set Mum's mind at rest.' She blushed again. 'And his intentions are honourable, even if that does sound a bit old-fashioned.'

'It sounds nice, love, and so does Joel,' said Ashleigh, patting her sister's hand. 'I feel sure I'm going to like him.'

And as she dressed for dinner later Ashleigh hoped fervently that she would like Joel Denison. For it was obvious that Gemma adored him. If everything her sister said about him was to be believed he was the nearest thing to perfection that you could find anywhere. And to think she had thought the detestable Mitch Patrick was her sister's fiancé! Well, all she could say was thank goodness he wasn't!

Mitch Patrick was the type of male whom she had always given a very wide berth. He had that aura of the dominant, the oh-so-sure-of-himself, keep-the-little-woman-in-her-place kind of attitude. Ashleigh could feel her hackles rise just thinking about him, standing looking down his arrogant nose at her. And if he had to pick her up from the airport you'd think he could have made some attempt to change from his working gear!

He must be employed in some capacity by the Denisons, even though he said he was related to Joel. A poor relation—Ashleigh quirked one eyebrow at herself in the mirror. Somehow she couldn't see the mighty Mitchell Patrick taking orders very easily from anyone.

Absently she picked up her brush and ran it lightly through her thick fair hair which shone brightly beneath the overhead light and curled neatly under at the ends to frame her face. She eyed herself critically. Gemma's statement that her oldest sister was beautiful was a gross exaggeration, she thought. It was a pleasant enough face, as faces went, with high cheekbones, a firm chin, large dark blue eyes fringed by long fairish lashes which she had darkened tonight with a little mascara, but hardly a face to set the world on fire. Frowning, she considered her lips. They looked tight, unused to smiling. But she often smiled when she was at home with the family, relaxed.

Jonathan's face swam before her, as they had parted the evening before. His scowl had taken her completely by surprise when she had told him she was flying up north to see Gemma. And she couldn't stop the thought that when she was with Jonathan they rarely laughed together.

'I think you're being far too over-protective, Ashleigh,' he'd said sternly. 'Gemma's old enough to live her own life and I don't think she'll thank you for running up there to see what she's doing.'

'That's not the reason I'm going, Jonathan,' Ashleigh had replied quietly. 'Mother's worried about Gem getting engaged. I'm merely going up to meet her fiancé, find out what he's like and set Mother's mind at rest. Apart from that I'd like to see Gem, if only for a few days.'

'Your mother's worrying unnecessarily. The whole trip is a waste of time and money. I'd appreciate it if you reconsidered and didn't go, Ashleigh.'

'My ticket's already booked and paid for and I've told Mother I'll go. I can't back out now.'

'Ashleigh, our wedding is only a little over three weeks away. You know we want it all to flow smoothly, and to have everything run like clockwork we have to plan and recheck all the arrangements.' Jonathan's scowl had deepened.

'I've got everything under control,' Ashleigh began, and sighed. 'Jon, I can't not go now.'

His expression had not relented. 'I certainly hope that when you become my wife your family won't think they can still make inroads into your time, sending you here and there as the whim takes them.'

'Don't be silly, Jonathan!' Ashleigh's hackles had risen. 'My family make no more demands on me than the members of any other close family would. Besides, we're all more than happy to help each other out when necessary. That's how we are.'

'Well, when we're married you won't have much time for helping out.' He glanced at his wristwatch. 'And talking about time, I'll have to be going. I've an important meeting in the morning, so it will be impossible for me to get away to drive you to the airport—since you insist on taking this ineluctable trip,' he finished sarcastically.

'That won't be necessary. Adrie and Vicki will be taking me out to the airport. Mother's coming, too. I'll be back some time on Wednesday afternoon.'

'Yes, well, give me a ring when you arrive and I'll try to get free to collect you.' He had kissed her perfunctorily on the cheek, not noticing her coolness, leaving Ashleigh in a turmoil of mixed feelings—irritation, guilt, uncertainty, and an overriding sense of frustration.

Voices in the living-room of Gemma's flat brought her out of her reverie. Her future brother-in-law must have arrived. Ashleigh stood up and smoothed her dark blue dress over her rounded hips, the shirred bodice neatly moulding her full breasts, and the sleeveless style was some deference to the warmness of the evening.

Now to meet Joel Denison and give him the once-over on behalf of the Craig family. Ashleigh's face broke into a smile and two large dimples appeared in her cheeks, making her look so much younger than her twenty-eight years. Although she was unaware of it, her smile did add a lot of credence to her sister's statement that Ashleigh was the beauty of the family.

And the smile still lit Ashleigh's face as she walked in to join Gemma. Joel was there all right. However, he hadn't come alone. Mitch Patrick paused as he stepped through the doorway, arms full of cartons of take-away food. Ashleigh felt her smile fade and knew by the tightness that appeared around his mouth that Mitch Patrick was more than aware of the fact that she was not ecstatic about his presence.

'Come and meet Joel, Ash,' Gemma was saying quietly, and Ashleigh turned from Mitch Patrick to be introduced to Gemma's fiancé.

Tall, with darkish hair and a humorous mouth, Joel Denison was a very personable man, nice-looking without being too handsome.

'Hello, Ashleigh. Gem's told me so much about you it's a wonder your ears weren't continually burning,' Joel smiled.

Ashleigh smiled back, liking him immediately. 'I hope she abridged some of it.'

'Oh, it was all good. I haven't heard Gem say a bad word about anyone, have I, love?' He put his arm around Gemma's shoulders and gave her a squeeze.

'I seem to remember a rather obnoxious boy who lived near our place . . .' Ashleigh's dimples danced in her cheeks.

'Oh, Ash, you wouldn't tell Joel about that!' Gemma blushed painfully.

'No, your secret's safe with me.'

'Could be interesting by the sound of it,' Joel laughed, and turned to the other man as he moved farther into the room. 'Oh, sorry, Mitch. You've met Ashleigh, haven't you?'

The fair head was inclined mockingly. 'I certainly have,' he said in that same deep voice, that played such havoc with Ashleigh's nerves. 'Miss Craig.'

If the blatancy of his rugged maleness this morning had rubbed Ashleigh the wrong way then his appearance tonight caused her even more discomposure. She became aware of the quickened beating of her heart, the way her nerve ends seemed to tingle as though he physically touched her where his eyes moved over her. And his eyes did rove over her with that same familiarity that set her teeth on edge.

The dark brown slacks he wore emphasised the narrowness of his hips, the muscular strength of his long legs, the overall lithe animal grace of him. His fair hair looked almost white beneath the light and it was neatly brushed, still damp from his shower, curling over the collar of his pale blue body shirt.

'Wasn't it lucky that Mitch could go out to the airport to collect Ashleigh?' put in Gemma quickly, sensing all was not well with her sister.

'Mitch is always available for an attractive girl, aren't you, mate?' Joel slapped his cousin on the shoulder. 'The only other guy I've ever met who can draw as many females to his side is Ryan.'

'I think I'm on my own now,' laughed Mitch. 'Ryan seems to be quite happily tied and hobbled.'

'Ryan's my older brother,' Joel told Ashleigh. 'He and his wife Liv are very happily married. They've got two great kids and another on the way.'

'And don't tell me, Mr Patrick,' Ashleigh remarked silkily, 'you have no intention of being tied and hobbled yourself.' Her eyes fixed somewhere about the top button of his shirt.

'How did you guess?' he replied, just as smoothly. 'Why buy a hat when there's plenty of shade from tree to tree?' he added outrageously.

Ashleigh's chin rose with unreasonable anger. After all, what did she care about his life style? 'Oh, I see. Not game to make a commitment?'

His eyes duelled stonily with hers. 'Oh, I make commitments of a sort where necessary,' he smiled cynically, 'but I always stipulate their,' he paused, 'flexibility.'

Ashleigh saw Joel and Gemma exchange a quick glance.

'Yes, well, let's eat dinner before it gets cold,' said Joel. 'Hope you like Chinese food, Ashleigh?'

Dragging her stormy eyes from the cynical twist of Mitch Patrick's mouth, Ashleigh turned to Joel with as much of a smile as she could muster. 'That sounds fine, thanks, Joel.'

'Great! Gem cam dish it out while I take care of the wine. Pass those glasses, will you, Mitch.'

Gemma's small dining table barely seated the four of them and to her consternation Ashleigh ended up between Gemma and Mitch Patrick. As he passed various dishes across the table his knee moved to touch hers, quite purposefully, she was sure. The heat of a

physical attraction seemed to radiate from her. It was a
feeling she hadn't experienced for years, since those
rapturous months with Robbie, in fact, and for a
moment she was disconcerted, and moved her knee
from contact with him, her eyes flying startled to his
face. A mocking smile, as though he knew of her attraction to him, expected it and it amused him, lifted
the corners of his sensual mouth. Ashleigh's anger rose
to almost choke her and she had to force herself to
remain calmly seated, to follow the conversation that
flowed about her.

'Did you manage to finish servicing the Cessna,
Mitch?' asked Gemma.

'Yes. I'll take her up for a test flight tomorrow. Not
that it's strictly necessary, but I'll use any excuse to
get in the air. I'll do a quick fly over the islands.'

The smile he gave Gemma unnerved Ashleigh once
again, and begrudgingly she had to concede that he
had more than his share of animal magnetism. All this
went to prove that he was a dangerous person to asso-
ciate with, Ashleigh warned herself. Although why she
felt she had to caution herself about anything where
Mitch Patrick was concerned she refused to analyse.

'Why not take Ashleigh with you?' suggested Joel,
and in horror Ashleigh's eyes flew from his across to
Mitch Patrick. A large airliner was one thing, and the
smallish plane that took them on their second leg from
Mackay to Shute Harbour had been bad enough. But a
small Cessna was another story altogether—especially
confined in one with Mitch Patrick.

'Oh, no, I couldn't,' Ashleigh burst out, trying to
calm herself. 'I . . . I came up to see Gemma, so I'll
. . . we'll just sit and gossip, catch up on all our news.'

'But you'll have to see something of the place, won't

she, Gem?' Joel turned to his fiancée. 'The Whitsundays are incredibly beautiful, and seeing that there's no time to take you sailing then flying over the reefs and islands is the next best thing.'

'I'd love to see it all but—well, Gem and I haven't seen each other for months, and besides, I'm sure Mr Patrick doesn't want to be bothered with a tourist jaunt.'

'On the contrary, I'd be pleased to take you along.' He leant back in his chair regarding her with that same amused, cynical knowingness.

Ashleigh's eyes appealed to Gemma for assistance.

'Actually, Ashleigh isn't very keen on flying,' put in Gemma quietly.

'What don't you like about it?' asked Joel sympathetically. 'Do you suffer from airsickness?'

'No, not exactly.' Ashleigh searched her mind helplessly for a valid excuse.

'Not frightened of flying with *me*, are you, Ashleigh?' Mitch Patrick smiled his provoking smile.

'Of course I'm not frightened of flying with you,' Ashleigh replied shortly, asking herself what would give her more cause for fear. Flying? Or Mitch Patrick?

'Then I'll pick you up after lunch,' he said blandly, and it was all settled.

'It really is magnificent from the air, Ash,' said Gemma apologetically.

'And later in the afternoon you can come over to our place for dinner. I'll collect you both when I finish work,' said Joel happily. 'My father's looking foward to meeting you. He wants to assure you that I'm a fine upstanding member of the community, a man any sensible girl would snap up,' he laughed, then looked at

Ashleigh with sincerity. 'I mean to take good care of Gemma, make no mistake about that, Ashleigh.'

'I can see you will, Joel,' replied Ashleigh softly.

'Yes, my cousin Joel here is considered to be the most eligible bachelor in the district—handsome, rich,' put in Mitch Patrick with wry amusement.

'Now that the most eligible bachelor is spoken for will you be putting yourself forward into the vacancy?' Ashleigh's blue eyes turned innocently to meet his. 'Or don't you feel you quite match up to the necessary requirements?'

His mouth formed the semblance of a smile, but she thought his eyes contained a flash of anger. 'Oh, I don't know. I'm eligible, and a bachelor, but it would take some woman to coax me into forfeiting my freedom, I can assure you of that. I'm afraid I'm a rather singular person in the main.'

'Well, I do trust that the hopeful females of the district are aware that you're a non-starter,' smiled Ashleigh, 'it would be such a waste of their time and energy.'

'I'm not saying I'm not open to the odd spot of cajoling,' he replied easily. 'Always mutually enjoyable, I feel. And to date I haven't been short of the occasional bit of female companionship.'

'No, I can see you would have a certain amount of appeal to some females.' Ashleigh couldn't recall being goaded to such rudeness before and was slightly ashamed of herself.

He laughed then, a deep sensuous sound that stirred long dormant feelings deep within her. 'Dare I take that as a compliment, Ashleigh?' he asked softly, his eyes narrowed, regarding her languidly.

'What else, Mr Patrick?' Ashleigh smiled back,

trying to control the tremble in her lips as the darkness of his eyes teased suggestively.

'What else indeed?' He turned to Gemma, who was sitting slightly disquieted. 'Your sister has a sharp tongue, Gemma. Is she a confirmed manhater, or is it just me?'

'Oh, I'm sure Ashleigh doesn't dislike you, Mitch,' said Gemma quickly, 'and she doesn't hate men at all. Why, she's getting married quite soon.'

'To a man, one of the dreaded enemy?' His eyes alight with a mocking glow went back to Ashleigh. 'He must be a man of outstanding personality and perserverence. I'd like to meet him.'

'Oh, Jonathan's very nice-looking,' Gemma put in as she watched the sparkle of anger light her sister's eyes. 'He's very distinguished and—er—conscientious,' she finished.

'No doubt I'll meet him at the wedding, Ashleigh,' Joel added smoothly, putting his arm protectively along the back of Gemma's chair. 'I'll also be meeting your parents as well, so I'm looking forward to that.'

'And to meeting the rest of the family,' laughed Gemma, relaxing. 'There's quite a tribe of us.'

'If you and Ashleigh are any example of the beauty of the Craig girls, perhaps I should have bided my time until I'd met the whole lot before making a decision,' Joel teased, and they laughed, lightening the atmosphere. 'I must say I admire your father's resilience, being surrounded by eight women.'

'Dad adores being the centre of attention,' laughed Gemma. 'Besides, he has three sons-in-law, with another two to come, to back him up now.'

'Let's see—three plus two, that's five. My arithmetic tells me you have two sisters left.' He turned to Mitch.

'There you are, mate. There's still time.'

Mitch laughed.

'He'll have to wait a while,' smiled Gemma. 'Louise is eighteen and Debbie's only twelve.'

'Oh, no,' said Mitch smoothly, 'if I can't have Ashleigh I'll just have to learn to live alone.' His eyes danced over her flushed face.

CHAPTER THREE

'WHY not simply tell him you're afraid of flying?' suggested Gemma. 'He won't press it, Ash. He's really quite nice when you get to know him.'

Ashleigh's look did not express belief.

'He is—truly,' nodded Gemma. 'I mean, it's not his fault that females throw themselves at his head all the time.'

'Do they? Well, there's no accounting for taste,' remarked Ashleigh sarcastically.

'Don't you think he's good-looking, Ash?' asked Gemma. 'Although I much prefer Joel's quieter good looks I can see his attraction—you know, big, blond and powerful. Usually all the girls vie for his attention.'

'Well, this is one who won't be,' she replied firmly, refusing to admit it was said more for her own benefit than her sister's.

'That's probably why you appeal to him, Ashleigh.'

'Appeal to him?' Ashleigh spun around from the window to frown at her sister. 'We can barely tolerate each other!'

'Then why do you both watch each other when the other's not looking?' Gemma laughed. 'Joel noticed it, too. He said it was a great pity you were already spoken for, because he could see Mitch meeting his match in you.'

'Did he now? And there was I thinking your Joel was very astute,' said Ashleigh, feeling a rising spurt

of excitement that confused her. Just the mere sugges-
tion that Mitch Patrick could be interested in her
caused her to tremble inwardly with a sense of anticipation. After all, she was twenty-eight years old, not
an unsure teenager. And on top of it all she had only
met the man yesterday!

'Ash, you do like Joel, don't you?' Gemma's serious
eyes were on her, her face a picture of consternation.

'Oh, Gem, of course I do. He's very nice. It would
be hard to dislike anything about him,' Ashleigh
assured her, sitting down beside her sister. 'You
couldn't have chosen anyone nicer. And neither could
Joel.'

Gemma shook her head, tears on her lashes. 'I'm so
lucky, Ash. I love him so much. I just can't wait till
we're married. But I guess you know how it is.' She
wiped her eyes. 'You and Jonathan have waited for so
long. You must be really excited.'

Excited? Was that honestly how she felt? Ashleigh
asked herself. She had been looking foward to her
wedding, to being married to Jonathan. Of course she
had. Had? Why should she choose the past tense?

She gave herself a mental shake. This was ridiculous!
Until yesterday she had been happily without reserva-
tions. Her life had been moving along planned lines,
along a course she had been quite satisfied to follow.
Now she was asking herself all these upsetting soul-
searching questions. And for what reason? Because a
supposedly attractive man has shown he could be interested in you, answered a small voice.

Ashleigh frowned, annoyed with herself. It had
nothing to do with Mitch Patrick. She had been thinking along dissatisfied lines on the plane yesterday
morning, long before Mitch Patrick strode into her life.

Perhaps Jonathan's unsympathetic attitude about her trip up here had set the ball rolling. And her over-reaction to Mitch Patrick was all just a progression from those few disquietening thoughts.

So he was an attractive man. She would simply treat him as she would any other attractive man. She would recognise that attractiveness for what it was and take him as a cousin of Joel's, nothing else. Tomorrow she would be back in Brisbane and Jonathan's solid conventionality would reassure her, would wipe away all this uncertainty. Perhaps it was only natural for her to feel this way. Pre-wedding jitters, didn't they call it?

'I think I hear the Range Rover,' Gemma brought her back to the present. 'Look, Ash, don't go up in the plane if you don't think you can take it.'

'I'll be all right, love. And I would like to see the Reef.' Ashleigh stood up and walked to the window, repressing a shiver of apprehension as she watched Mitch Patrick spring lithely down from the cab and stride towards her. She could imagine how he would laugh if she admitted her fear of flying. Well, even if she had to close her eyes she would fly with him. She wouldn't give him the satisfaction of refusing. 'Besides, I want to take my camera and get a few shots to show my class next year,' she added as she went to open the door.

'Ready?' he asked with a half smile, his eyes amusedly letting her know he expected her to decline his offer to take her with him.

'Yes, I am,' she told him with deceptive calmness, and slung her camera bag over her shoulder.

'Good. See you in a couple of hours, Gem,' he said, and turned back towards the car.

Ashleigh followed, hurrying to keep up with his long

purposeful strides. He wore blue jeans, faded in parts, which hung low on his hips, the flared bottoms accentuating his height. His broad, muscular shoulders were clearly moulded by the matching shirt that fitted in to his narrow waist. He'd rolled the long sleeves up and they fitted snugly over the muscles in his upper arms and his fair hair, shining in the sunlight, lifted gently in the breeze. Too handsome altogether, Ashleigh thought wryly.

'I did have a small feeling of doubt that you'd come along, Ashleigh,' he remarked as they drove out to the airfield. 'You didn't seem overly enthusiastic last night.'

'I'd be silly passing up the chance of seeing the Great Barrier Reef from the air, wouldn't I?' she replied casually.

'Yes. I must admit it's a sight worth seeing.' He glanced at her, his expression amused. 'Even worth spending a couple of hours with me, wouldn't you say?'

Ashleigh could feel her features tightening and took a steadying breath. She mustn't let him goad her. 'I'll have to wait and see, won't I?'

He laughed outright at that and in exasperation Ashleigh gave her attention to the roadside, wishing now that she had refused to come. And she would be wishing it continually, she had no doubt, as the afternoon progressed. If she was going to have to contend with his baiting as well as her tremulousness at flying in a small plane then she was not looking forward to the next few hours.

They completed the rest of the short journey in silence and Ashleigh managed to refrain from making a scathing remark about the mocking smile that lifted the corners of his mouth each time she caught his profile in the edge of her vision. He was the most arrogant, self-opinionated, irritating man it had ever been her misfortune to meet!

'There she is,' he said as he pulled the Range Rover in beside a large corrugated iron shed. The size of the little single-engined aircraft didn't strike much confidence in Ashleigh's heart and she felt the familiar quiver of dread begin dancing in the pit of her stomach.

'I imagined it would be bigger than that,' she remarked to cover the feeling of horror that must surely be reflected in her eyes.

'It's adequate as two-seaters go. Very intimate, in fact,' he smiled, almost purring with amusement.

Reluctantly Ashleigh followed him across to the little orange and white Cessna.

'Let's get aboard. Here you are. Mind the step.' His hands went around her waist and Ashleigh almost slipped in her haste to escape the sensations those strong brown fingers evoked. She sensed he knew it, too, and refused to meet those dark, mocking eyes.

By the time they were both seated in the aeroplane Ashleigh's mouth was dry and she could feel the churning in her stomach begin to intensify. The cabin was so small and Mitch Patrick was far too close for her peace of mind. She fixed her eyes on the panel of dials and gauges, not seeing them, wishing she could swallow her infernal pride and break out of the small confined space.

Her eyes sprang on him in fright as his body leant across and his hand moved in front of her. Her muscles tensed, but he was only reaching for her seat-belt and as he fastened it his hands touched her, burning through the denim of her jeans, the soft terry towelling of her loose blouse. The blood began to pound along Ashleigh's veins, beating in her head until a thin film of perspiration broke out on her brow.

She raised an unsteady hand to wipe it away, but he had turned aside, fastening his own seat-belt, switching switches, adjusting. And then the engine came to life.

Ashleigh clutched convulsively at the sides of her seat, swallowing the panic that rose inside her, as she felt the beat of the engine through her body. What a fool she had been to come! She'd never conquer this fear. Why did she put herself through it? She opened her mouth to ask him to stop so that she could get out, but he was speaking into a microphone, taxiing out on to the runway.

In no time they had left the ground and were climbing steadily into the brilliant blue of the sky. Not that Ashleigh saw any of it; her eyes were tightly closed.

'Ashleigh?' His voice came from somewhere, echoing in her ears.

She swallowed painfully, still sitting rigidly, eyes closed.

'Ashleigh?' His voice was louder this time and she moved her mouth to answer him, but her throat refused to open and no sound came out.

His hand on her arm brought her eyes open at last and she slowly turned her head to look at him. All the amusement had been wiped from his face as he took in her paleness, the clammy coldness of her skin.

'Why the hell didn't you tell me you felt like this about flying?' he demanded harshly. 'We'll turn back straight away.'

'No!' The word broke out of her. 'No! I'll be all right in a minute. I'm . . . I'm not sick. I just have to get used to it. Don't go back.'

'Look, we'll be up here for some time. There's no point in suffering for nothing,' he said with a little less harshness.

'No, really. I . . . I'd like to see the Reef and I've . . . I've brought my camera. I just have to get acclimatised.' She made herself move her head to gaze out over the view of the incredibly beautifully coloured blue water and the scattered green splashes of the islands. Unconsciously she moved closer to the inside edge of the seat.

Mitch Patrick's hand tightened momentarily on her arm and she looked back at him. His eyes locked with hers, a flicker of something she couldn't quite fathom in their dark blue depths. He released her, saying something under his breath that sounded imprecatory, and returned his attention to the plane.

'As you like, Miss Craig,' he said drily, and they began to lose a little height so that he could point out the various islands. They journeyed in silence for some time and gradually Ashleigh began to lose some of her tension.

'Whitsunday Island to your left is the largest island in this group. It's a National Park and the highest peak rises some four hundred and forty metres.'

The colours in the tableau that lay below them was breathtaking and before Ashleigh knew it her fear was replaced by sheer ecstatic pleasure. Taking out her SLR, she clicked away, wishing she had a movie camera so that she wouldn't miss one tiny section of the beauty.

'The next island there is Craven,' Mitch leant over to indicate the direction. 'It belongs to Joel's brother, Ryan. The hotel's up the far end and Ryan's built himself a house just off the beach there. See it in the trees?'

Ashleigh nodded. 'It's . . . it's quite a successful resort, I hear.'

'Very much so. Hasn't been in operation quite twelve months yet and Ryan's more than pleased with the response. He gives genuine value for money and he seems to have the knack of knowing just what people want. When you combine that with sound business acumen—well, it can't help but be successful.'

'Does Joel have any part in the island?' she asked, her mind caught up in the blue water, green palms, white sands.

'No. It's entirely Ryan's baby.'

The sharpness in his voice drew her eyes back to his face.

'But don't be distressed, Miss Craig.' The mocking smile was back. 'Joel's quite wealthy in his own right. Didn't I say he was the district's most eligible bachelor?'

Anger at the meaning behind those cynical words whipped colour into Ashleigh's cheeks. 'Joel's wealth would have been the last thing Gem would have considered,' she said testily.

He smiled crookedly. 'But it helps.'

'Do I detect a faint colouring of sour grapes, Mr Patrick?' Ashleigh asked sweetly.

The smile vanished from his face and his fine fair brows arched together. 'The hell you do,' he retorted, and then he seemed to take his anger in hand and one eyebrow lifted mockingly. 'Maybe you've misjudged me, Ashleigh. For all you know I could be one of Australia's wealthiest men. It might be to your advantage to cultivate me just in case.'

'Thanks. But no, thanks,' Ashleigh looked back to the view. 'I'm quite comfortably off myself. I've no aspirations towards acquiring more money.'

'But I'd make an educated guess that the prospective Mr Ashleigh Craig is not poverty-stricken.'

'Jonathan Randall,' she emphasised his name, 'is financially comfortable. Not that it's any business of yours,' she added shortly.

He laughed again. 'Should I show my bank statement?'

Ashleigh ignored him, raising her camera to her eye, framing another shot.

'We're moving down to the southern end of the Whitsunday Passage,' he said after a while. 'The passage is about thirty kilometres long and quite wide. Its minimum width is three kilometres.'

'Look at the extent of the coral reefs surrounding that island,' Ashleigh remarked. 'The colours are indescribable! There's every shade of blue you could imagine, right through to a deep purple.'

Mitch circled lower. 'The section immediately below water level on the outer edge of the coral bank is where the most attractive coral growths are to be found.'

'Is it any wonder conservationists feel the Reef should be guarded so diligently?' Ashleigh mused.

Mitch looked at his wristwatch. 'We'd best be heading back. I'll take you out a little farther to the ocean edge as we go. Pity we can't stay longer, but I don't like the look of those clouds gathering on our landward side.'

Ashleigh gave the fluffy whiteness a desultory look before once more giving her attention to the blue below, and it was some time before she realised that Mitch Patrick had fallen silent. She glanced across at him, sensing a watchfulness, and she tensed in her seat.

Catching her glance, he motioned towards the mainland. The white cotton wool of a short time ago was now a solid bank of grey white heavy cumulo-nimbus and the turquoise blue water was changing colour dramatically.

'Will we ... must we go through it?' Ashleigh asked.

'No. We'll have to put down and sit it out,' he replied without expression.

'Put down?' she repeated in disbelief. 'But where? There's only the water!'

'I'm making for an island I know. We'll land on the beach and there's a small shelter of sorts there. I've used it before.' He spoke easily, as though he was discussing an everyday trip to the supermarket.

'Can't we go over the storm? Or maybe around it?' she asked, forcing a wave of fear down inside her.

'No. We wouldn't make it around, it's moving in on us too quickly,' he replied. 'And even if we got up over the top of it we still have to go down through it to the airfield. There's the island now.'

Ashleigh looked down and her stomach lurched in fright. 'You can't mean to try to land on that narrow strip of sand?' she got out huskily, thinking she wouldn't have put it past him to conjure up the storm.

'It's the only thing we can do. The beach is wider than it looks from up here.' He glanced at her pale face. 'Look, Ashleigh, flying into cloud like that over there is asking for trouble. Visibility would be absolutely nil and I could very easily lose my orientation and fly straight into the sea.'

As he spoke he was dropping off their height, and

Ashleigh clutched her seat as the island drew closer.

'Hang in there, Ash.' His face broke into that same cynical smile. 'I told you I'm going to enjoy getting to know you better. I don't intend losing you now, so you're in good hands.'

The main wheels touched the hard sand with a slight bump, the speed of the aircraft still relatively high, and he eased forward on the controls to allow the nose wheel to make contact with the ground. As they rolled along the beach he braked cautiously, aware of the uncertain condition of the surface, and they had almost stopped when the nose wheel sank into a patch of soft sand. Almost in slow motion Ashleigh felt the aircraft nose down, throwing them forward against their seat-belts. The propeller hit the sand and as the plane lurched Mitch was thrown to the side, cracking his head on the windscreen pillar.

The abrupt silence almost screamed in Ashleigh's ears and her hands reached out to him in agitated panic.

'Mitch! Mitch! Are you hurt? Are you all right?' She could feel her voice rise higher, bordering on hysteria. Her hand touched the side of his face and came away damp and red and she struggled against the restrictions of her harness, the heaviness of her suspended weight. 'Mitch?' His name came out on a sob.

His dark eyes opened slowly, blinked, and then the vagueness cleared. The crooked smile swept one side of his mouth upwards and he took hold of her hand as it rested on the side of his face. 'If I'd known it would only take a crack on the head to get you to call me Mitch I'd have arranged it sooner,' he said huskily, sending the blood pounding through Ashleigh's veins as she snatched her hand away.

'How can you make detestable jokes at a moment like this?' She felt so angry she could have hit him.

'I think we'd better use some of that pent-up energy getting you out of here,' he said. 'Otherwise you might be inclined to finish me off.'

Climbing down from the plane sitting at that angle was not the easiest thing to do, and by the time her feet touched the sand Ashleigh thought her legs would give way beneath her. She clutched at the side of the plane for some support and then strong arms came around her, holding her close. Her hands slid naturally against the hardness of his chest, taking some comfort from his solidness and strength.

Her eyes went to his face, moved from the fullness of his sensual lips, rose to gaze into the depths of his eyes as blue as sapphires and then were drawn to the ragged gash that had opened on the side of his face at about the height of his cheekbone. Most of the blood had dried on his face, but his exertions climbing out of the plane had opened the cut and a slow trickle of red had started to ooze from the wound.

At the sight of it Ashleigh's command snapped. Tears filled her eyes and spilled over to course down her cheeks and she tried to turn her head away from him. He lifted his hand to his face and felt the wetness, and he looked down at her, his mouth wearing that infuriatingly cynical smile. Although his eyes had narrowed, his thick fair lashes shielded their expression.

'Those tears aren't for me, are they?' he asked, and put his lips softly to the dampness of her cheek. 'No one's ever cried for me before.'

'Oh, Mitch!' Ashleigh whispered, almost overcome by her awareness of him, of his strength, of the strong sure beat of his heart beneath her hands, and her fingers curled into the thick denim of his shirt.

His arms drew her closer, his lips descending until they found hers, touching softly, moving away, to return, each gentle caress drawing all Ashleigh's pent-up responses to throb within her, and her lips trembled, following his as he drew away and finding them again until his kiss hardened, demanding a response she gave him of her own volition. Ashleigh's whole body tingled, her senses honed to fever pitch, her blood pounding through her body in abandonment.

The strong hardness of his thighs filled her with such a tide of wanting she couldn't contain the half sob, half moan that escaped from her lips. His own lips had trailed molten fire down to the softness of her throat, his hand reaching up from the roundness of her hips to cover one full breast. Oh, to be able to sweep aside the outside world, her ordered mundane even flowing life, and let herself drown in the newness of this soaring ecstasy.

'God, Ashleigh, this is a hell of a time to . . .' his lips were drawn back to the line of her jaw and went upwards to kiss her eyelids. 'To hell with the time,' he murmured thickly, and went to claim her lips again.

Through a mist of her own heightened passions Ashleigh could feel him beginning to let his control slip and a feeling of panic took hold of her, sweeping passion aside, causing her to push against him, and she stumbled back against the plane as, taking him by surprise, she broke from his arms.

Their eyes met, locked together, neither of them able or capable of looking away. Mitch's eyes narrowed and his lips tightened. He let his gaze fall down over the agitated rise and fall of her breasts before giving a cynical laugh and turning away to pick up the canvas bag he'd dropped out of the plane before they climbed out.

'We'd better get to the shelter before the rains come,' he said flatly.

'Mitch, I'm sorry,' Ashleigh began, and he turned to face her. 'I'm not in the habit of . . . I mean I don't . . . It was just reaction after the . . . the crash,' she stammered.

The crooked smile was back. 'Miss Craig, you're giving my ego a beating! And I thought it was my irresistible technique,' a slight note of sarcasm had entered his voice. 'Let's head for the shack. It's going to pour any minute and I want to come back and secure the plane.' Without looking at her he began striding over the sand.

Ashleigh started after him, her legs shaking. The hut was just inside the first row of low bushes, and when he'd said it was a shelter of sorts that was just what he'd meant. The roof was covered in a type of thatch, perhaps of palm leaves, and there were no covered walls.

'It's mostly waterproof,' he said, 'and the rain will just fall straight down. Joel and I built it a couple of months ago when we had to land another plane with a spot of engine trouble.' He put the canvas bag under the hut and stepped back out to Ashleigh. 'I won't be long. I'll have to secure the plane as best I can. With a bit of luck the rain will hold off for me.'

'But your face——' Ashleigh began.

'You can play doctor when I come back,' he said, and taking one of her hands he raised it to his lips and kissed it nonchalantly. 'And I was so sure you wouldn't be overly concerned if my life's blood trickled away. More surprises! Is there a glimmer of hope for me, Ashleigh?' He raised one eyebrow and disappeared back towards the aeroplane.

It was some time before Ashleigh moved, and when she did her legs still felt rubbery. She sank down on to the sandy floor of the shelter, one hand resting on the canvas bag Mitch had left there.

The whole of the afternoon before they landed on this island seemed to have faded into insignificance. The flight. The reefs. All that filled her mind was their embrace on the beach, those few passion-packed moments when she was in his arms and the world stopped.

Her whole body trembled as she recalled her own part in the interlude. If he now thought her free and easy, a pushover, then who could blame him? A tide of shame at her abandoned behaviour washed over her. To think that she allowed herself to forget her fiancé, their coming marriage, all that it stood for, for just one stolen moment! Her hands clutched together as the remembered pressure of Mitch's hard body had her senses reeling again.

He was such a physical animal, she told herself, and she was unused to that. Any woman would have felt an attraction to him. His looks were in vogue—big, blond, rugged, so much the macho man. And hadn't he said himself that he did not want for female companionship? He would draw women like bees to honey, and she'd just joined the queue.

Oh, yes, she could well imagine what he was thinking. Congratulating himself on another conquest ready for the taking, most likely. Well, if he thought that then she would have to prove him wrong! She had repelled any advances made to her in the past. Why should Mitch Patrick be any different? Perhaps he was a little more physically attractive, but that was all. As a person, he left her cold.

Does he? asked a mocking voice inside her. You only have to think about him and you fall to pieces. You're putty in his hands. What a fool she was! She was acting like a naïve inexperienced adolescent. If this went on she would be unable to face Jonathan when she returned home tomorrow.

Home! Heavens, Gemma would be frantic when they failed to return! It would be dark in a couple of hours and then they'd have to spend the night here. How long would the rain last? Perhaps it would clear. As that thought crossed her mind the first spots of rain began to fall in giant blobs, kicking up puffs of white sand where they fell to earth.

Where was Mitch? She stood up and walked across to the edge of the shelter. Should she go after him? Perhaps he needed help with the plane? Visibility as the rain fell was considerably reduced, and Ashleigh screwed up her eyes as the upturned tail of the plane began to fade into the curtain of water.

As she hovered uncertainly she caught sight of Mitch sprinting up the sand. He was drenched, his shirt dark and sticking to him, his fair hair plastered on to his head. He put one hand up to dash the hair and water from his eyes—and at that moment he slipped and sprawled his length on the sand.

Not stopping to think, Ashleigh bounded out from under the shelter and was beside him in a dozen strides. He had pushed himself on to all fours and her arms went around him, helping him to his feet. His hands still clutching her for support, he shook his head and she thought she heard him swear.

'I must have fallen in a blasted hole. You should have stayed under the shelter.' He had to shout above the roar of the rain. 'Come on, we're soaked through!'

They made a mad dash for the hut, and it was only as she stood out of the torrent that Ashleigh realised how cold the rain was. The temperature had fallen drastically and her teeth began to chatter as she squeezed a rivulet of water from her hair.

Mitch pulled the press studs open down the front of his shirt and struggled out of it, wringing it out and hanging it over a part of the rude framework of the hut. His muscles glistened with drops of rain as he bent down to the canvas bag, his jeans squelching water.

'Should be a towel in here somewhere,' he said, pulling out a couple of dark grey blankets. He stood up, towel in hand. 'Here, rub your hair dry.'

Ashleigh did as he said and then returned the towel to him and he gave his own hair a vigorous rubbing. 'You'd better get out of those wet clothes,' he said evenly, and began to unbuckle his belt.

A dull flush crept over Ashleigh's face as her eyes flew open wide. 'If you think I'm . . .' She stopped, turning angrily away from him as he unzipped his jeans.

'Don't be a fool, Ashleigh. There's no telling how long this downpour will last and while there's no wind, there's still been a considerable drop in the temperature. It's ridiculous to catch a cold when there's two perfectly dry warm blankets to wrap ourselves in.'

She could feel him peeling the wet denim over his legs and then he was squeezing water from them. Her heartbeats began to skip, accelerating to throb in her throat.

'No need to be modest at a moment like this.' His voice was amused. 'I have seen a woman's body before,' he laughed, 'on more than one occasion.'

'But you haven't seen mine,' Ashleigh retorted. 'And what's more, you're not getting the opportunity to see it!'

'In those wet clothes I'd say I could see quite a bit of it. Every delectable contour is very nicely moulded.' He moved around until he was in front of her.

Unable to stop herself, Ashleigh looked down over his broad chest, the hard flatness of his stomach to the brief underpants he wore and flew back to his face in embarrassment. He began to rub the moisture clinging to the fair curling hairs on his chest and Ashleigh had to restrain herself from reaching out to touch him, to run her hand over his firm tanned torso.

She became aware that his own eyes had moved down to where the wet terry towelling of her top snugly moulded her breasts, and she turned her back on him again, disconcerted and angry. 'You're being rude!'

He chuckled again. 'You can turn around now, Miss Craig. I'm properly wrapped in a blanket to save your maidenly blushes. I'll even turn my back while you strip. That's making a supreme sacrifice to show my good faith!'

Ashleigh heard him move away and turned slowly around. He was down on his haunches, wrapped in a blanket, sorting through the kit. Nervously she began to untie the lacings at the front of her shirt and then she quickly dragged it over her head, holding the towel protectively in front of her. Her lacy bra was saturated as well and she slipped out of it, one eye on Mitch's back. But he showed no sign of looking in her direction.

It took some time for her to remove her jeans. They clung to her and she only had one hand free to pull them off. The other hand clutched the blanket about her. When Mitch heard her wringing her clothes out he turned around amusedly, watching as she hung them up alongside his.

'What did I tell you? I bet you feel warmer already. A cup of soup will warm you even more.'

Ashleigh walked across to him in surprise. He'd set up a small spirit stove and on the top a small can of water was beginning to boil away.

'All mod. cons., madame,' he grinned, and opening a sachet of dried soup powder he poured it into a tin cup, added the hot water and passed her the steaming liquid.

She took it from him, her tummy tumbling emptily as the aroma teased her nostrils. 'What about you?'

'I'll use the billy.' He emptied the dried soup into the can and sat down opposite her on the sandy floor. 'It's only soup and dried biscuits, but it's better than nothing.' He raised his cup to his lips. His hair stuck out from his head in unruly strands, already beginning to dry, falling on to his forehead in waving disorder. He turned his head to offer her a biscuit and she saw the jagged cut on the side of his face.

'Oh, Mitch, I haven't dressed the cut on your face. Is there a first aid kit in the bag?'

He lifted a small box bearing a red cross. 'After we've finished dinner,' he motioned with his makeshift cup. 'It'll last out till then. It's stopped bleeding.'

'What about the storm? Do you think it will last much longer?' Ashleigh asked, her hands getting welcome warmth from the hot cup of soup.

Mitch shrugged. 'The cloud was pretty thick, but the storms are usually shortlived, even if they do empty the heavens in that short time.'

'But will you be able to get the plane righted on to its wheels so that we can get back?' Ashleigh had to suppress a shudder at the thought of taking off from the strip of beach.

He paused before answering. 'Depends,' was all he said.

'On what?' asked Ashleigh.

He shrugged again. 'On a number of things.'

When he didn't appear to be going to expand his answer her anger rose. 'Look, Gemma's probably frantic by now, not knowing where we are.' A thought struck her. 'The radio! We could use the radio in the plane to send them a message and let them know we're okay.'

'I tried the radio,' he said flatly.

'Did . . . did it work?'

'I hope it did.'

Ashleigh took a deep steadying breath, suppressing an irritated desire to slap him. 'What do you mean you hope it did?'

'I couldn't receive, but I think I got a message out before it went dead. If not,' he lifted one hand in a resigned gesture, 'we'll have to wait until I can get back to the plane to repair the set.'

Ashleigh's face was pale. 'Wasn't there any way you could tell if someone heard you?'

He shook his head. 'But Joel will guess that I'd head for this island.'

'What about the plane? Can we fly out when the rain stops? I mean, even if it's dark.'

Grinning crookedly, he shook his head again. 'I'm afraid we're here for the night, Ash.'

CHAPTER FOUR

'You can't mean that,' Ashleigh said softly.

'Yes, I do. I may not be able to get out of the soft sand. And if the tide comes in that far, which it probably will, it will be even worse getting her out. And even supposing we do manage to right the plane the propeller took quite a knock, so it could very well be bent.'

'You're . . . you're teasing me,' Ashleigh breathed.

Mitch gave her an infuriating grin. 'I could give you the names of a dozen girls who'd be ecstatic to be in your position, stranded on a deserted island with me— all alone, just the two of us.'

'My God, you're the most egotistical, self-opinion-ated . . .'

'Now, now, Ashleigh, that's not nice.' He was clearly thoroughly enjoying himself. 'I consider myself lucky to be here with you. A jug of wine,' he raised his can of steaming soup, 'a loaf of bread,' he indicated the dry biscuits, 'and thou.' His eyes held hers mockingly. 'And we're high and dry as well. What more could we ask?'

Ashleigh couldn't trust herself to speak. Standing up, she turned her back on him, clutching the blanket about her.

He laughed again. 'Come on, Ash. We have to make the best of it.' When she didn't move he stood up and joined her. 'Look, I apologise for teasing you, but you leave yourself open for it. What do you say we try to call a truce for the next few hours?'

Ashleigh's eyes met his and he looked genuinely serious.

'Truce?' He raised his fair eyebrows.

Ashleigh sighed. It seemed there was nothing to be done about the situation. She could hardly fly the plane out herself. 'All right,' she said flatly. 'But I don't care to be baited all the time.'

Mitch inclined his head. 'Sit down again and we'll try to pick some mutual subjects to discuss to pass the time. Believe me, Ashleigh, Joel will reassure Gemma. He knows I wouldn't take any risks. Okay?'

Ashleigh nodded and they finished their soup in silence. It didn't take her long to see to the cut on his face. Although it was ragged, the rain had cleansed it and all she could do was gently tape the edges together.

'I think it may have to be stitched. You might have a scar there,' she told him, his nearness playing havoc with her senses again.

'If we hadn't called a truce I might be inclined to remark that my handsome face has been well and truly ruined,' his eyes smiled into hers, 'but I won't, of course.'

Ashleigh reluctantly laughed with him and put the first aid box back into the canvas bag.

'Gem said you were a teacher,' he remarked at last.

'Yes. A primary school teacher,' Ashleigh replied. 'This year I had a class of eleven-year-olds. Quite a responsive group, too, so I feel I've had a good year.'

He nodded. 'Sounds like you enjoy your work. Been teaching long?'

'Yes, I love it. And eight years,' she replied, and his eyebrow rose in surprise.

'You don't look old enough to have been teaching that long,' he said, and raised his hand as she gave him a sceptical look. 'No, you don't. I wouldn't have put you more than three or four years older than Gemma.'

'Thank you,' she said with tongue in cheek. 'I'm twenty-eight. There's three sisters between Gem and me. I have the doubtful honour of being the eldest in the family.'

'At the risk of sounding trite, you sure carry your age well.' He grinned easily at her, his eyes dancing over her face.

Ashleigh's heart was behaving peculiarly again. There was the smile he used on Gemma. His face held none of the cynical mockery she had seen on it more often than not and his genuine smile added to his potent attractiveness. He really was devastatingly goodlooking.

'What about yourself?' she asked a little breathlessly.

'Oh, I'm an old man of thirty-five,' he replied, and Ashleigh laughed.

'No. I mean what do you do for a living?'

He paused before answering, his smile fading slightly, and she thought she saw a flicker of something she couldn't define reflected in his eyes. 'I'm rather a jack of all trades. At the moment I'm flying tourists over the reefs and back and forwards to some of the larger islands. I'm working with D.J.'

'D.J.?' Ashleigh repeated.

'Joel's father, D. J. Denison. He started the tourist operation in this area. He has quite a monopoly on it and until a few years or so ago he ran the show pretty well singlehanded.'

'But didn't Joel and his brother work with him?'

'D.J.'s been a bit of an autocrat in his time—ruled everyone with an iron rod. Ryan cut out and was away for some years and it was only after he returned and bought Craven Island that D.J. mellowed a bit and let go the reins somewhat. He's turned most of his organisation over to Joel and although he keeps interested he has more time now to devote to his political aspirations. Old D.J. feels strongly about this area, wants to preserve its natural beauty as far as is possible. He'll do it, too. He has a healthy group of supporters around these parts.'

'He sounds quite formidable,' Ashleigh put in, and Mitch laughed shortly.

'He's rather strong-minded. Guess it runs in the family.' He set his empty can on the sand, not looking at her. 'My mother's D.J.'s sister.'

'You don't mean to say that your mother is as awesome as D.J., do you?' Ashleigh smiled.

He looked at her then and his cynical smile was back. 'Oh, she's like D.J., only more so.'

Sensing something running below the surface of his words, Ashleigh regarded him steadily, wondering whether she should pursue the subject or let it drop. But Mitch took the decision out of her hands.

'If you haven't already guessed, I'm considered to be the black sheep of our side of the family.' He had slipped back into the half amused, half cynical attitude that had rubbed Ashleigh the wrong way when she'd first made his acquaintance.

'And what exactly have you done to earn that title?' she asked, trying to bring back the lighter side, wanting to see the relaxed, uncomplicated Mitch Patrick of not long ago, thinking he could be quite likeable when he forgot his bored and cynical pose.

'Oh, this and that,' he laughed. 'Both my mother and D.J. feel it's the duty of the firstborn son to take over the family business. No matter what.'

'And you're the firstborn son and you don't want to take over the family business,' remarked Ashleigh.

'And I don't want to take over the family business,' he repeated.

'Why not?'

'Because I'm not a farmer.'

Ashleigh couldn't help smiling at that. 'No, I must admit that you don't look like one either.'

He pulled a face at her. 'To add insult to injury, my twin brother, younger than me by half an hour, is at one with the earth, a very good farmer, so to speak.'

'You mean there's two of you? Let loose in the one district?' Ashleigh found herself enjoying this new lighthearted relationship and the dimples danced in her cheeks. 'Poor girls!'

He smiled back, his gaze moving over her face, his eyes dark and unfathomable. 'Yes, I'm afraid there's two of us. Plus two sisters, both married, and one younger brother still at school.'

'And is your brother—the farmer, I mean—is he tied and hobbled?'

Mitch paused again and then shook his head. 'No. No, we're both available. Choice of two.'

Even though his answer was amused Ashleigh sensed again that he simply skimmed the surface, that there was something more that ran much deeper. 'Is your brother like you?'

Mitch raised his eyebrows.

'I mean, is he self-opinionated, conceited, chauvinistic and—er—other such adjectives?' Ashleigh grinned.

'Not the way you mean,' Mitch laughed outright at that. 'Matt's pretty much an exact opposite. We're not identical twins.'

'Mmm. Perhaps you could introduce me to him, then,' she chuckled. 'I'm sure I'd like him.'

'I'm sure you would,' he said drily, and she thought his mouth tightened momentarily. 'Anyway, that's enough of me. What about you?'

'Very boring, I'm afraid,' Ashleigh shrugged. 'As I said, I'm a teacher who enjoys teaching.'

'And is your fiancé a teacher as well?' Mitch was watching her through half-closed eyes.

'Jonathan?' Ashleigh said his name as though it was unfamiliar to her. It all seemed so far away somehow. She mentally shook herself. 'No. Jonathan's an accountant,' she said quickly.

He nodded, still watching her. 'Have you known him long?'

'Almost . . . about eight years.'

'That's a long time. How come you didn't marry sooner?'

'Jon . . . that is, we wanted to be sure and—well . . .' Ashleigh felt herself flushing, wondering why she was feeling so defensive about it.

'You shouldn't marry him,' he said with a lack of tact, in an arrogant tone that put her back up.

'I shouldn't marry him,' Ashleigh repeated sarcastically. 'Oh, well, I wouldn't dream of marrying him, then. The great Mitch Patrick has spoken!'

Their easy camaraderie of a moment ago had vanished as though it had never been.

His lips tightened at her taunt. 'It's true,' he said evenly. 'If you can wait eight years you don't want to get married badly enough.'

'I suppose a person like you couldn't understand that some people like to work towards a goal, wait until they're ready financially and emotionally to make a lasting commitment.'

'Commitments again, Ashleigh?' he said sardonically. 'All this talk of committing sounds very much like sentencing. To a person like me, that is.' He moved closer to her. 'Nothing lasts for ever, Ashleigh. Surely you've learnt that? You have to take the moments when they're there, otherwise you could wait your life away. Like you've been doing these past eight years, you and good old Jonathan. He must have ice water in his veins.'

'You've no right to criticise Jonathan! You don't even know him. And you don't know me.' Ashleigh seethed, a picture of Robbie flashing into her mind. She and Robbie hadn't had time to . . .

'Oh, but I do.' His tone had dropped, assaulting her vulnerable senses with its sensual huskiness. 'And I'd like very much to know you better.' His eyes went to the rise and fall of her breasts beneath the blanket sarong. 'Be sure it wouldn't take me eight years to do it either.'

'I'm afraid I need more in a relationship than the purely physical.' Ashleigh clutched at what calm she had left.

'Don't knock the physical,' his eyes settled languidly on her lips. 'Not until we've tried it.' He raised one eyebrow suggestively. 'Or have I hit on the reason for Jonathan's lack of haste to make an honest woman of you? Is he having his cake and eating it too?'

Ashleigh was almost speechless with anger. 'You are, by far, the rudest, crudest, most obnoxious . . .' she spluttered.

'Physical individual?' he finished, totally enjoying himself. 'But you didn't answer my question, Ashleigh.'

'And I don't intend answering it either. My sex life is my business.' She looked away from him, completely disgusted. 'Your family must have been relieved to see the back of you!'

'But the girls in the district miss me,' he said softly.

'I'm tired of this conversation. You don't seem to be able to stop yourself bringing everything back to sex,' she retorted, angry with the persistent throbbing of her own body.

'Don't you like sex, Ashleigh? Is that the trouble between you and Jonathan?' he laughed softly, watching her like a cat teasing its prey. 'Maybe he doesn't have the right technique.'

Ashleigh stood up facing him angrily, her temper flaring, recognising some slim thread of truth taunting at the back of her mind. Jonathan's caresses had always been pleasant, but they had never lifted her to any great heights. Even Robbie's lovemaking had . . . But she had been young then, and intense.

'And I suppose you have,' she threw at him, then chastised herself severely. That was all but an invitation for him.

'Maybe I have.' He stood up slowly, in one fluid movement. 'You won't know until you try.'

The thought of Mitch Patrick making love to her made her freeze with shock. Her body wanted it, craved for it, but in her mind she held herself in check. If he touched her she knew she'd be hard-pressed repelling him. At all costs she must see that he didn't realise the effect he had on her. Her eyes met his. He was so sure of himself, so provokingly masculine. How she'd love to strike his ego down to size!

'I think you overdo it, Mitch,' she said silkily. 'Could it be you feel you're not as good as you'd like to be. You know the old saying? Self-praise, etc.' Ashleigh smiled.

'You play with fire, Ashleigh. Aren't you afraid you might get burned?'

He had moved closer, stood within a foot of her, and Ashleigh flushed, the spark of his physical magnetism reaching across to bridge the distance, touching her vulnerable senses, emphasising the fact that those long-dormant senses lay so very close to her outwardly calm exterior.

With a superhuman effort she stood her ground. 'I'm sure it would take a better man than you to melt me, Mr Patrick.' As soon as the words were out Ashleigh could have bitten her tongue.

His laugh had her stepping backwards, but of course, he was far too quick for her, his hands going out to close over her shoulders, strong fingers propelling her nearer, until her body was against his. 'My, my, so provocative, Miss Craig! What red-blooded Australian male would refuse to take you up on that? I'm going to enjoy proving you so very wrong.'

Ashleigh's hands pushed against the rough blanket covering his chest. 'Let me go, damn you!'

'You don't mean that, Ash, so why say it?' His lips touched her cheek as she turned her face aside from his descending mouth. His fingers captured her head then, holding her lips exactly where he wanted them, and his eyes bored into hers as he slowly lowered his head. She knew what to expect, knew that the kiss would be punishing, for she read it in the dark blue depths of his eyes. She had insulted his manhood and

he was extracting his price, his mouth an assault on
the softness of hers. Ashleigh fought him, but he
turned each movement she made to his own advantage
until their embrace was neither punishment nor con-
frontation, and Mitch's hands strayed down the
responding nerves in her spine, down to cup the
roundness of her hips, to pull her impossibly closer to
the hard contours of his body. And somehow
Ashleigh's hands had slid upwards, unconsciously
sensuous as they roved over the taut muscles in his
shoulders and neck, her fingers insinuating themselves
in the damp disorder of his hair.

It was as though they had both been waiting, burning, to continue the embrace they had shared on the
beach. Now the steady beat of the rain, the rustle of
the undergrowth, the hundred different sounds in the
swiftly falling darkness faded into nothingness, millen-
niums away, as they floated in a cocoon of timeless,
earth-shattering ecstasy.

Ashleigh moaned softly as Mitch's lips teased her
earlobe, moved down to the whiteness of her throat,
and she buried her head in his shoulder, running her
tongue over the smoothness of his firm muscles. Her
fingers pulled at the edge of his blanket and it fell away,
her hands then moving over the softness of the fair
curls on his chest before sliding around to the breadth
of his back. His lips found hers again, gently probing
the inner sweetness, and only when the cold air
touched her almost naked body did she realise he had
stripped her blanket from her. Standing back a little,
he gazed down over her breasts, the roundness of her
hips clad only in scanty bikini briefs, and she heard
him draw his breath before his hands reached out to
caress her, cupping each firm breast, stimulating the

sensitive nipples until she moaned and swayed towards him. His arms crushed her to him, the damp hardness of his chest exquisite delight.

'Ashleigh,' he murmured gruffly into the mat of her almost dry hair. 'You're a witch—you have to be. You're casting a spell around me and I'm damned if I even want to try to escape.'

Closing her eyes, Ashleigh almost fainted at the wave of pure desire that rose within her. How she wanted him, wanted him more than she'd ever physically wanted anyone in her life before. She ached for fulfilment, her fingers moving feverishly over his firm flexed muscles.

She didn't realise he had laid her on one of the blankets until his legs moved over hers, his body as aroused as her own. In the semi-darkness his eyes burned brightly and she put her hand up to the roughness of his cheek. He closed his eyes, almost agonizedly, and turned his lips to kiss the palm of her hand. Leaning on one elbow, he ran his hand over her breasts, down the contours of her midriff, her flat stomach, stopping at the line of her briefs. His lips slid along her jawline and she wound her arms around his neck, her fingers in his hair.

'God, Ashleigh, I want you like crazy,' he murmured in her ear. 'Every single beautiful inch of you.'

'Oh, Mitch!' His name came out in a voice she scarcely recognised as her own. 'It's never been like this for me before. I'm so glad you're the first.' Her hands trembled on his body, began to pull him back to her. 'Love me,' she murmured against his lips.

He began to kiss her again—and then abruptly the cold air struck between them, causing her to shiver.

'Mitch?' She moved closer to him, her breast brushing his arm, her body arching towards his.

'Say that again, Ashleigh,' he demanded.

'What? Say . . . say what again?'

'About being the first.'

'It's true,' she said. 'I've never . . . Don't you believe me?' Her hand went to his arm and he flinched away. 'Mitch?'

He sat up and drew his legs up under his chin, breathing deeply, his back to her.

Ashleigh was unable to move. She lay where he had left her, the pain inside her burning deeply. How could he think she'd lie to him about that? 'Mitch, please, I . . . I want you to be the first.' Her hand moved involuntarily to the bulging muscle of his forearm.

'God, Ashleigh, don't do that! I'm a man, not a bloody stone statue,' he said harshly. 'And I'm so close to crossing the line that I don't trust myself so just leave me be for a while—unless you want to take the consequences.'

Eventually he turned back to her and a flicker of pain crossed his face. 'You'd better tie yourself up in that rug before I change my mind,' he said thickly.

Ashleigh sat up then, his words a douche of cold water on her body and her arms covering her breasts, her face flushing red with shame, shame at the hollow feeling of disappointment that sat heavily upon her.

'God, I could use a cigarette,' he muttered, and stood up, scooping his own blanket from the sand where Ashleigh's agitated fingers had cast it.

'Mitch?' Ashleigh began, and swallowed hoarsely. 'What's the matter?'

'You can ask that?' He spun on her. 'You can't be that naïve, Ashleigh? And even you with your low opinion of me, even you couldn't imagine I'm that big a bastard!'

She stared across at him, her eyes large in her face.

Running his hand distractedly through his hair, he shook his head. 'I'll spell it out for you. I've been around, as the saying goes, and I haven't lived the life of a monk. I told you before, you have to take the moments when they're there, and I've taken what was available from females who knew the rules, knew the score.' He looked at her, his jaw tense. 'And you haven't even got a cross on the board!'

'Don't you want to make love to me?' she asked him quietly.

He ran his hand over his jaw, as though to relieve some of the rigidity. 'Oh, I want to make love to you, make no mistake about that. I want you so badly it's an ache inside me. But I'd hate myself afterwards.' He gave a harsh laugh. 'I must be bloody mad! Or that bump on my head did more damage than I thought it did.' He sighed. 'You'll thank me, Ash, when you walk down the aisle in your white dress to good old Jonathan. Now, you'd better get some sleep.'

'Where are you going?'

'To the plane for my cigarettes.' He picked up a torch and flicked it on. 'And maybe a cold swim,' he said with self-derision, and disappeared into the night.

CHAPTER FIVE

FOR long minutes Ashleigh stood and watched the bobbing circle of light from the torch Mitch carried as it moved away from her. She found it impossible to make her body react to the signals her brain sent out. She was totally numb, emotionally and physically, and she welcomed the deepening darkness. Somehow her shame was just bearable in the enveloping blanket of the night, away from the unrelenting daylight.

The rain had stopped, she realised, and she shivered as the cool night air, fresh from the downpour, crept about her naked body, and she slowly knelt down and searched the sandy floor for her discarded blanket. Her fingers found it, shook it out and thankfully drew it around her.

Get some sleep, he'd said, but sleep was the last thing on her mind. The way she felt at this moment she doubted she'd ever sleep again. Would she ever be able to forgive herself for her actions tonight? Every time she closed her eyes the whole bitter-tasting scene would replay in her mind, torturing, humiliating. And how would she be able to face him in the hard light of day? It wasn't as though she could escape him, stranded as they were on this tropical island.

Lying on the sand, Ashleigh drew her knees up as she cringed in agony. She could hardly believe she had acted so out of character. She had all but begged Mitch to make love to her. All her self-respect had been lost, her pride had been cast aside, in fact she'd acted like a frustrated, weak-minded, naïve ... There weren't enough adjectives, there weren't any strong enough to describe her foolishness. And she would never be able to forget the wretchedness she was feeling at this moment.

Squeezing her eyes tightly closed, she prayed for the oblivion of sleep. But as if she had not suffered enough Jonathan's face sprang into her mind and a wave of self-revulsion swept over her again. Her guilt ate away at her, a physical pain inside her.

How could she just return to Brisbane now and go innocently about finalising the arrangements for their wedding? How could she stand beside Jonathan and make her vows? For she had been unfaithful to the trust Jonathan had in her, perhaps not the ultimate physical perfidy, but the fact that it wasn't had been no fault of hers. She would have given herself to Mitch Patrick without a single solitary thought for her fiancé—and that was unforgivable.

When she went back she would have to tell him, try to explain the whole sordid incident, and if he wanted to sever their engagement then she wouldn't be able, in all honesty, to blame him. Jonathan was a man of high principles, and he had thought that she was equally honourable.

Honourable? Ashleigh almost laughed. It seemed that there is a little of the dishonourable, the immoral in all of us, she sneered at herself. Her thoughts flew back to those whirlwind months she shared with Robbie. She had been about to surrender herself to him and whether or not she would have gone through with it was something she would never know. But it proved one thing. She didn't like this weakness in herself very much, and it would be a long time before she would be able to come to terms with herself again.

Mitch Patrick. Her lips twisted in the darkness. What cruel trick fate had decreed that their paths should cross at this particular moment in time? A time when she had been so comfortably satisfied with her life and its direction. She had been so sure that she would have made Jonathan a perfect wife. But now . . . Even if he did forgive her, did want to go through with their plans, could she trust herself to play the part of the kind of wife Jonathan wanted? Who was to say that in a month, a year, five years after her marriage, she might meet another Mitch Patrick and be drawn by his physical magnetism?

Finally Ashleigh dozed off, sleeping fitfully through the long night. Much later she heard Mitch return and settle himself under the shelter, but she kept her breathing regular, although her heartbeats seemed to echo in the darkness.

First light brought her slowly from sleep and, half awake, she stretched languidly, easing her aching muscles. The air was a little humid and she pushed the blanket aside, blinking at the grassy roof above her for some seconds bevore she realised where she was. The island. The plane. Mitch Patrick!

Her eyes flew to the other side of the shelter. He was stretched out, leaning casually on one elbow, looking perfectly at home, his gaze on her, falling lower, taking in the full rise of her breasts. Ashleigh clutched the blanket over her, her face hot with colour, unable to meet his eyes.

'Don't tell me you're shy, Ashleigh?' he said, his amusement tinged with an edge of sarcasm. 'Forgotten I've seen you like that before? Considerably more of you, actually.' One fair eyebrow rose.

'Would you mind going outside while I get dressed?' Ashleigh drew on all the self-possession she could muster, her voice almost steady.

He smiled at that and lay back, hands beneath his head, his own blanket low over his narrow hips. 'I'm quite comfortable here, thanks.'

Ashleigh glared at him, her anger rising. 'If you had any manners, any decency at all, you'd . . . you'd do as I ask you!'

'But, Miss Craig, that would be the last thing someone like me would do. One minute you've got me tipped as a blackguard, the next a knight in shining armour. I just don't know where I am.'

'Oh, you know where you are all right,' Ashleigh blazed back, 'so don't pretend you don't!' His mocking smile fanned the flame of Ashleigh's temper and throwing the blanket aside she jumped up and reached for her clothes. 'If you need a few cheap avaricious thrills at my expense, then okay, look your fill. But just let me tell you you are the most despicable contemptible creature it's ever been my misfortune to meet anywhere!' She tugged ineffectually at her jeans, still damp and stiff as a board.

He was beside her in a moment, anger blazing in his own eyes and his hands closed on her pulling her around to face him. 'Ashleigh, you'll push me too far with that sharp tongue of yours.'

'Take your hands off me!' she cried, almost falling with one leg only half in her jeans.

'Aren't we brave this morning?' he laughed, goading. 'Must be the good night's sleep you had. You did sleep well, didn't you, Ashleigh?'

'Yes.' Ashleigh managed to get out, the blood beginning to pound in her veins at the expression that

kindled in his eyes, her hands pushing ineffectually
against his chest.

'Well, I didn't,' he remarked huskily. 'I almost went
quietly insane lying here beside you, not touching you.'
As he spoke he drew her unresistingly against him, his
hands moving almost feverishly over her before his lips
came down desperately to claim hers.

The spark ignited immediately and Ashleigh
returned his kiss with unrestrained passion. That
mutual flare destroyed all her carefully built defences
with catastrophic ease, sweeping her up and along in a
deluge of desire. They were drowning in each other,
their hands clutching each other for support. Ashleigh
moaned softly as his lips found one sensitive spot after
another, driving her into a heady, sweet madness of
delight.

They both became aware of a loud droning sound at
much the same time and they stood together listening.
'Cessna,' Mitch said almost to himself. 'Must be Joel.'
He looked down at Ashleigh as though he would pull
her back into his arms. 'What a time to be rescued,' he
said unevenly, and Ashleigh pushed herself away from
him, her mind a jumble of incoherent thoughts.

She was unable to move, and almost mesmerised she
watched Mitch grab the striped towel they'd used the
night before and race out on to the beach waving it
about his head. She heard the droning sound grow
louder, as though the plane came lower, was preparing
to land. The thought of other people, other eyes,
touching the circle that encompassed the scene of their
passionate hunger threw her into a fever of motion.
She pulled her jeans up over her hips, struggling
against their still damp tightness, clipping the waist
stud with difficulty, for it seemed as though they had

shrunk overnight. Her shirt had fallen on the ground and she agitatedly shook the sand out of it before pulling it roughly over her head as she ran out on to the beach after Mitch.

The small aeroplane circled a couple of times and then began to drop off height as it came in towards the beach on the same path that they had landed the afternoon, eons, before.

'He's not going to try to land, is he?' Ashleigh shouted above the noise. 'What if he . . . what if he doesn't make it?'

'He'll make it,' he said, and turned a quizzical smile on her. 'If not there'll be three of us stranded.' He looked back to the plane, his hand shielding his eyes. 'As you were—four of us stranded. That could be Gemma with him.'

'Gemma!' Ashleigh's heart flew into her mouth as the small plane touched down. 'How could Joel bring her with him? And put her in danger landing on the beach.'

'Your sister probably saw more danger in you being here alone with me than flying with Joel,' he watched her face flush. 'And she had good cause, it seems,' he added quietly, beginning to walk towards the now stationary plane, wrapping the towel around his waist as he went, his tanned muscular shoulders glistening in the sunlight.

'You two okay?' asked Joel earnestly as he sprang down from the plane, looking from one to the other.

'We're fine,' replied Mitch. 'Scratched my cheek, but Ashleigh patched me up. Did my call get through, or was it an educated guess on your part that we'd be here?'

'Bit of both,' grinned Joel.

'Ash, are you sure you're not hurt?' Gemma's voice came agitatedly from the cockpit.

'Hang on, love, I'll help you down.' Joel strode around to open Gemma's door and lifted her down on to the sand. 'There, what did I tell you? Ashleigh's fine. Can't see a mark on her,' he laughed as Gemma turned to her sister.

Over Gemma's head Mitch's eyes met Ashleigh's and she flushed at the thoughts she knew were passing through his mind. No, she thought, there wasn't a mark on her. There was nothing to show that his hands had caressed her body, that his lips had seared a trail of sensual agony, that his body had been moulded to hers with exquisite ecstasy. The bruises and scars were not on her body but were nevertheless etched deeply on her seemingly vulnerable heart.

'They picked up part of your radio message at Craven Island,' Joel told Mitch. 'At least they heard enough to know you were safely down, but they didn't catch where. Ryan rang me and I was just about sure it would be here.'

'Oh, Ashleigh, I was so petrified for you!' Gemma closed her eyes. 'I didn't know what to do. In the end I rang Mother and she did a back-flip. I had to get Joel to talk to her and eventually he convinced her you would be safe. But if we hadn't got the radio message . . .' she shuddered. 'Joel, we'll have to let Mother know.'

Joel patted her shoulder. 'We'll get a message back. I knew Mitch would look after her.'

Ashleigh almost laughed aloud. Oh, he'd looked after her all right! Her eyes brightened with anger as they met his and the cynical smile that briefly touched his mouth didn't help her at all.

'Did you hit a patch of soft sand?' Joel asked as they walked over to the other Cessna.

'Yes. I don't know how I failed to see it,' he said, 'unless I had my eyes on Ashleigh instead of the beach.'

Both men chuckled goodnaturedly while Ashleigh longed to slap the two of them.

'Very understandable,' replied Joel. 'Shouldn't take us long to get it back on its feet,' he grinned. 'Think the prop will be okay?'

'Hope so. We'll check it all out, but I don't see that it would be bent, we didn't hit down very hard, just tipped slowly up. I switched off the engine when I felt her going.' Mitch bent down for a closer look. 'I'll go back to the shelter and get dressed and we'll get stuck into it.'

Gemma's eyes went over Ashleigh's creased clothes. 'It looks as if you were soaked through. I hope you don't catch cold.'

'We ... we got wet getting to the shelter,' said Ashleigh, feeling herself flush again. 'But Mitch had a couple of dry blankets and a towel.'

'You must be starving. I've brought some sand-wiches with me.' Gemma began limping back to the plane.

'I'll get them down.' Ashleigh went with her. 'You shouldn't even be walking on that leg.'

'Oh, Ash, if it had been broken I wouldn't have stayed at home. I knew I'd be frantic until I could see for myself you weren't hurt or anything. I just wouldn't let Joel go without me.'

Ashleigh unwrapped the sandwiches as Mitch rejoined them, his bare chest glistening in the sunlight. He'd rolled his jeans up at the bottom and they clung as tightly on his hips as Ashleigh's did.

'Either I've put on weight or my jeans have shrunk,' he said, 'I had as much trouble putting them on as you did yours, Ashleigh.'

Gemma's eyes grew round and went from Mitch to her sister and over to Joel, an embarrassed blush washing her face. Ashleigh's eyes fell away from Gemma's and, mortified, she wished the sand would open up and swallow her. Didn't he realise how that had sounded? Her eyes flicked over him and she saw the amusement on his face. Damn him! Of course he knew how it sounded. He'd said it on purpose.

'I'll radio back to Craven Island that you're both safe and get Liv to ring Ashleigh's mother,' Joel said quickly, climbing up to the cockpit of his Cessna. He stopped halfway in and turned back to Gemma and Ashleigh. 'Why don't you two go up to the shelter, get out of the sun. It could take us some time to check the plane over.'

'We'll be all right, Joel. We can sit in the shade of the wing,' said Gemma. 'And watch you two at work.'

'Okay,' replied Joel. 'As long as it's not too hot for you.'

Between the two of them Mitch and Joel pulled the plane back on its wheels and then set about checking for damage. They spent a lot of time on the propeller and spinner, removing the nose cone and inspecting it before screwing it back in place. Then they checked the cowling, the wheels and wings before starting on the engine, and when Mitch finally stepped up into the cockpit both Ashleigh and Gemma stood up waiting for the engine to fire. When it caught Joel gave Mitch the thumbs-up and turned to smile at the girls.

Shutting off the engine, Mitch climbed down and

both he and Joel crossed to the other plane.

'Good news, girls,' said Joel. 'Everything seems to be in good working order. We'll be home for lunch!'

Ashleigh looked over at the plane and her stomach lurched. How could she climb back into that plane, into the confined space of the small cockpit again, after the horror of their forced landing? She felt a thin film of perspiration break out on her brow.

A firm hand went around her shoulders and the warmth of Mitch's hard body beside her penetrated the numbing coldness.

'How about collecting our gear from the shelter, Ashleigh, while we get Gem back into the other plane.' His voice was deep and quiet, his hand moving her in the direction of the hut before she had time to think about it. Almost zombie-like, she crossed the hot sand of the beach and began to pack everything into the canvas bag.

'You have to get back into the plane, Ashleigh.' His voice behind her startled her and she dropped the mug she had just picked up.

Her eyes met his and then slid away. 'I don't think I can,' she said flatly.

'I know you can.' He took the canvas bag from her fingers and turned back to the beach.

Ashleigh stood her ground, her breath tight in her chest. When she didn't move he walked back to her, standing facing her, barely inches from her, and his hand went to the back of her head as she looked up at him.

'Where's all the fire now, Ash?' His voice was soft, so assertively physical. 'I thought you'd be pleased to get away from the seclusion. And me.' His lips came down on hers with a gentleness that twisted painfully inside her.

'Let's go,' he said, and took her arm, moving her on to the beach and towards the plane. He opened the cockpit door and turned to her.

'Mitch . . .' A sob caught in her throat.

But his hands were around her waist and he propelled her upwards, leaning inside, unravelling the harness and fixing it firmly about her, his hands brushing her tense body, tantalising her senses, changing the freezing timbre of her tension. She sat back in the seat and closed her eyes, her hands clasping the buckled harness. His hand covered hers for a moment and then he had closed the door and disappeared around the front of the plane before reappearing beside her, settling himself into his seat.

The engine came to life and Ashleigh jumped, her eyes opening in time to see Joel lift his Cessna off the sand and climb into the blue of the perfect sky. Mitch set the 150 after him, and soon Ashleigh felt the lifting sensation and slowly opened her eyes again. With painful slowness she forced her body to relax, her hands, her elbows, her legs.

'How long has flying affected you like this?' Mitch's voice broke in on the concentration she was exerting on her tensed muscles.

'It always has,' she replied. 'I'm not very fond of precipitous heights either. Perhaps I fell out of my cot when I was a child.' She tried for lightness.

'Perhaps you did,' he laughed. 'Well, after this you should find the large jets child's play.'

'Talking of large jets, I'll have to see if I can get a seat for tomorrow's flight. My tentative booking for today has left without me.' Ashleigh kept her eyes on Joel's plane to her side of them.

'You'll be able to enthrall your grandchildren with your tale of spending the night marooned on a tropical island,' he said, his voice teasing. 'And what will you tell them about me, I wonder?'

'What makes you think I'll even recall your face?' Ashleigh remarked, not able to stop her eyes from moving over his strong chiselled profile, suspecting wryly that his face was etched somewhat deeper on her memory than she cared to admit to herself.

'Oh, I think you'll remember me, Ash,' he said softly.

She tried to laugh it off. 'Only time will tell, won't it?' And as soon as she got back to Brisbane she would be able to put it all behind her, get back to normal. This couple of days would fade into the past, a dream, a fantasy.

'Shall we make a pact to meet in fifty years and see if we recognise each other?' he chuckled. 'On second thoughts, you might hit me with your walking stick.'

'I might, at that,' Ashleigh found herself laughing with him, warming towards him.

'And I might have to kiss you again to bring you under control,' he said.

The laughter froze in Ashleigh. The memories of their lovemaking were too new, too raw to be amusing to her. Lovemaking! she jeered at herself. Love had nothing to do with it. In the cold light of day it was all so cheap and low.

Her love had been given to Jonathan. What had flared between Mitch Patrick and herself was simply a physical reaction fanned by the heightened sensations of their dangerous landing on the beach and their isolation in the romantic setting of the hut, a warm and dry cocoon in the midst of a tropical deluge. Any two people would have been carried away by the situation.

In the same circumstances Jonathan would have . . . Ashleigh stopped. No, Jonathan would have been decorousness itself. There would have been none of the passionate kisses, the searing caresses, the will-destroying wanting that Mitch Patrick had evoked. And there would have been none of the self-despising heaviness of guilt that twisted inside her.

'Are you going to tell good old Jonathan about your——' he paused, 'escapade?'

His words thrust the knife-edge of guilt deeper and she turned on him, hating him, wanting to pierce that hard cynical egotistical shell, wishing she could find the chink in his armour, his Achilles heel.

'What makes you think I won't?' she retorted angrily. 'Jonathan is a fair-minded adult. He's kind and he's understanding and he,' she gulped a breath, 'he happens to love me.'

'Love has a habit of changing a level-headed adult into an evil-tempered, narrow-minded juvenile,' he said with his cynical smile in place.

'And you obviously are judging everyone by your own predictable reactions!' Ashleigh threw back at him. 'Jonathan will understand the situation, the circumstances.'

His laugh was harsh. 'He's either a namby-pamby or some sort of god. At least you'd get an honest reaction out of me, out of any normal man whose fiancée has made love to another man.'

'We did not make love!' Ashleigh's voice rose, a disquietening mixture of feelings surging within her—guilt, remorse. Regret?

'We might as well have done,' he replied. 'As far as Jonathan would be concerned, anyway. If I were you

I'd keep it to myself. Jonathan isn't going to understand the situation at all, take my word for it.'

'How can you judge how he'll react? You don't even
know him,' Ashleigh seethed. How could she ever have
thought him anything but the cold egoist that he was?

'No, I don't. But he doesn't sound your type,
Ashleigh.'

'You have a habit of generalising. Why do people
have to run to type?'

'Jonathan's not passionate enough for you,
Ashleigh.'

Her cheeks flamed as her mind filled with the picture
of her response to Mitch, the unity of their bodies
moulded together. 'My God, you've got some nerve!'
she spluttered.

'Look, Ashleigh, if you respond to Jonathan the way
you responded to me last night then no way would you
be stepping down the aisle in virginal white. Much of
that and you'd have a raving neurotic on your hands.
He wouldn't be able to keep his hands off you.'

'Jonathan is considerate and controlled. He . . . he
respects me.' She hated the feeling that she needed to
defend Jonathan, almost make excuses for him.

'Oh! Considerate, controlled, respectful,' he repeated
with ominous quietness. 'All that I'm not, is that what
you're trying to tell me, Ashleigh? Well, you've got a
hell of a short memory. You know, it never fails to
amaze me how often women practise self-delusion.'

'I'm not deluding myself about anything,' Ashleigh
retorted, too angry to notice they were losing height.

'Of course you aren't. There was no participation by
you in our little roll in the hay, or should I say sand?
It was all some figment of my depraved imagination.'
His voice was laced with sarcasm. 'Didn't you beg me

to make love to you?'

'Why, you despicable . . .' Ashleigh thought she had never been so angry in her life.

'Lost for words again?' He laughed harshly. 'Despicable maybe. But honest! Which is more than you're being with yourself. Maybe I was wrong. Perhaps you should be candid with good old Jonathan. At least it would kill or cure your relationship.' He stopped talking and Ashleigh felt the bump of the wheels on the runway.

Without another word he opened his door and sprang down from the cockpit. Before Ashleigh could undo her harness with her agitated fingers he was around at her door, taking her camera bag and depositing it on the ground and then returning for her. His eyes met hers, his dark and as unfathomable as parts of the waters they had flown over and hers clear and bright, whipped by her anger.

'Has good old Jonathan ever seen you with your eyes flashing like beacons?' he teased, his hand cupping her face.

'Take your hands off me, Mitch Patrick!' Ashleigh bit out, almost beside herself with anger.

His laughter rumbled deep within the solid wall of his chest, the sound all dominant self-assured male. 'Remember what I said about taking the moments when they're there? Well, this may be my last chance to kiss the bride, so . . .' His lips descended on hers, his fingers holding her face so that she couldn't turn away.

There was no gentleness in his kiss this time. It was all purely punishment, a potent demand for capitulation, and Ashleigh fought against the power he could exert over her, and somehow she knew she had lost the battle. When he finally raised his head the glow of victory gleamed in his eyes, sat on those sensual lips in a knowing smile that played about his mouth. Without stopping to think Ashleigh swung her hand and felt the sharp stinging contact with his face. The sound reverberated about the inside of the cockpit and, although the slap had lost a lot of its power as she was restricted in the small space, she could only feel horror at her actions. All trace of amusement had been wiped from Mitch's face and his lips thinned angrily.

'If you ever do that again I'll belt you back, Ashleigh, I promise you,' he said quietly.

'You deserved it!' She made a pretence of showing him he didn't intimidate her in the least.

'Why? Because I can pierce that frigid little pose, the disguise you don to cover the real Ashleigh Craig?' he said. 'It gets to you, doesn't it, Ash? That someone like me can make you forget to act the poised, self-assured female and can show you the passionate real woman underneath?' He laughed. 'I wonder if Jonathan realises what a bargain he's getting. Well, Ashleigh? Does he know there's an active volcano beneath the ice, just waiting to erupt?'

'You're crude and ill-mannered,' Ashleigh bit out, 'and I feel sorry for you. The only way you can understand anything is to bring it down to the physical. That's the limit of your comprehension, isn't it? Women aren't people to you, they're simply something to use for your own physical appetites. You may have pulled the wool over plenty of female eyes in the past, but I knew exactly what you were the first time I saw you!'

'My, my, and what was that?' His eyebrow rose with a tolerating kind of sarcasm. 'Don't stop there, Miss Craig.'

Ashleigh gave a soft laugh. 'Oh, they're called lots of things the world over. And I'll admit, in certain—er—circumstances you do have your, shall we say rather obvious uses, at which you're quite practised, I'll give you that. But after the lust fades away what's left? An empty nothingness. Now, would you please stand down, I want to get out of the plane.'

Eyes cold as steel, he stepped away and Ashleigh climbed out. His hands went around her waist, lifting her down, and with slow deliberation he turned her round, his hands on her waist, brown fingers spread firmly over her hips. 'You've got it all sorted out in that nasty little mind of yours, haven't you? Sorted out the way you want it to be, that is. Well, that's more self-delusions. You're a sensual woman, Ashleigh, you can't escape that. It's there inside you and if you were sensible you'd let it out instead of trying to close your eyes to it. Hell, Ash, it's nothing to be ashamed of.'

'I am not ashamed of anything!' Ashleigh's anger was on the boil and she was feeling better about slapping his face as the moments passed. 'Now, let me go.'

He shook his head and exclaimed in exasperation. 'Ashleigh, if I kissed you again you'd still respond. No matter how much your words deny it, your body gives you away.'

The edge of Ashleigh's sneaker-clad foot glanced off his shin and she had the satisfaction of hearing his gasp of pain as his hands fell away from her. 'Just keep your hands off me,' she bit out, and turned towards Joel and Gemma as they left their Cessna and began to walk across to join them.

'Bet you're glad to be back on firm ground, Ashleigh,' remarked Gemma, her eyes moving from her sister's set face to the unleashed anger Mitch was barely disguising.

'Yes, I can't say I enjoyed the flight one little bit,' Ashleigh replied, picking up her camera bag.

'How'd she go, Mitch?' Joel addressed his cousin, a flicker of amusement lurking in his eyes, making Ashleigh suspect he'd seen their brief exchange a moment earlier. 'The plane, I mean,' he added, breaking into a grin.

'No trouble at all,' replied Mitch. 'With the plane. Now Ashleigh's a different matter,' he said drily. 'Let's get home to a shower,' he flexed his muscles tiredly. 'Can't say I'd recommend sleeping on sand, no matter how congenial the company.' He began walking towards his Range Rover.

'Can you drop me off at the office on your way home, Mitch?' asked Joel. 'I've lent Gem my car till hers is fixed up so she can take Ashleigh straight back to the flat. As it's an automatic she won't have any trouble driving it with her bad knee.'

'Okay, let's go.' Mitch was all for a speedy departure.

'See you, Ashleigh, tonight at our place for dinner,' said Joel, giving Gemma a light kiss. ' 'Bye, love.'

Mitch had the engine going before Joel had seated himself and he didn't look back as he sped away, flinging gravel from beneath the tyres.

'Wow! He was in a hurry!' remarked Gemma, unlocking the door of Joel's neat little sedan. 'And in a temper.'

'Pity about him,' said Ashleigh shortly, seating herself in the passenger seat beside her sister.

'Oh, dear. Did you and Mitch have an argument or something?' Gemma frowned worriedly.

'Mitch Patrick is one big male chauvinistic argument as far as I'm concerned,' Ashleigh replied.

'But he's very nice, Ash. He can't help . . .'

'I know, I know. He can't help it if women throw themselves all over him,' Ashleigh finished for her. 'That's a pretty poor excuse for his ill manners.'

'Ill manners? But I've always thought he was well-mannered,' said Gemma. 'He always is with me.'

'Well, he isn't with me. And if he thinks I'm going to let him . . .' Ashleigh stopped and shook her head, not wanting to have to discuss Mitch Patrick's kisses with anyone. 'Anyway, I'll not be fussed if I never see him again.'

'But, Ashleigh, he got you safely to the island so you wouldn't have to fly into the storm, and—well, you should be a bit more grateful to him, shouldn't you?'

'Grateful?' Ashleigh pulled a face. 'Oh, yes, I'm jolly grateful. Grateful I don't have to spend any more time with him, that's all. The arrogant, self-opinionated, overbearing . . .' she stopped and shook her head.

'But, Ashleigh . . .' Gemma sighed. 'Oh, well, maybe it's for the best. I mean, Jonathan and—well . . .' She glanced apologetically at her sister and then started the car towards the exit.

Another wave of guilt washed over Ashleigh. She hadn't given Jonathan or his feelings a thought since they landed. He was probably waiting to hear she was safe—not to mention how frantic her mother would be.

'We'd better find a phone box, Gem. I want to check my flight back and then I'll ring Mother so that she knows first hand that I'm all right. Jonathan, too.'

Gemma nodded and pulled the car into the kerb.

'Mother? It's Ashleigh.'

'Oh, Ashleigh, I'm so relieved to hear your voice! We've been so worried, even after that very nice young woman phoned us this morning. She said she was Joel's sister-in-law. Oh, Ashleigh, we thought . . .' Mrs Craig's voice faded away.

'Now, Mother, don't upset yourself. I'm fine and none the worse for the experience.' Ashleigh smiled wryly to herself. And Mitch Patrick's kind of experience she could well and truly live without.

'I'm just so thankful you're safe,' Mrs Craig said tearfully. 'Your father's coming back this evening, thank heavens. I didn't realise how much I missed his steady calmness. When will your plane be arriving?'

'That's just the problem, Mother—I can't get a seat until Monday.'

'Monday? But, Ashleigh . . .'

'There wasn't one vacant seat available until then. You know this is peak period. I couldn't even get a booking on the bus,' Ashleigh explained. 'I'll ring you later in the week if the situation changes. Oh, and don't worry about Gemma. I've met Joel and he's exceptionally nice. Now, I'll have to go. I want to ring Jonathan.'

'Ashleigh, wait!' Mrs Craig cried agitatedly. 'Jonathan had to go down to Sydney yesterday with one of his clients and he won't be back until later this afternoon. He asked me to get you to ring him at home at eight-thirty. He's been worried about you, too.'

'Well, I don't know . . . I . . . You'd better ring him for me, Mother, in case I can't get to a phone. Oh, damn! there's the pips and I've no more change. I'll ring you again about my flight back. 'Bye, Mother.'

Ashleigh climbed back into the car beside Gemma, a frown hovering on her brow.

'What's up, Ash?' asked her sister. 'Mother's all right, isn't she?'

'Hmm? Oh, yes.' Ashleigh dragged her thoughts into some semblance of order. 'I think hearing from me has set her mind at rest as far as my being in one piece.'

'How about Jonathan?'

'He wasn't there. He's in Sydney. He left a message with Mother for me to ring him tonight at eight-thirty. Which I won't be able to do if we're going over to Joel's place for dinner,' she replied absently.

'Of course you'll be able to phone him. Joel's father won't mind you using his phone.'

'Long distance?' Ashleigh raised one eyebrow.

'You can always have them reverse the charges,' Gemma remarked as she pulled back on to the roadway. 'I'll ask Joel,' she added with the confidence of one who felt she could ask her fiancé for the moon and have it given to her forthwith.

They lapsed into silence, Gemma to concentrate on her driving and Ashleigh to mull over some disquietening thoughts. Irrational thoughts, she tried to tell herself. But no matter how she looked at it Jonathan couldn't have been too worried about her fate. After all, he had gone down to Sydney when as far as he knew, she had been lost in a small plane somewhere over the blue Pacific Ocean. If he really cared about her he would have been frantic, would have come in search of her.

Especially knowing she was with Mitch Patrick. But Jonathan hadn't known that, so it didn't apply. However, he must have known she'd be with a pilot. Her heart sank. Jonathan trusted her. And that was the whole point, wasn't it? If you loved someone you trusted them. She had complete faith in Jonathan.

Which was more than she could say for Mitch Patrick. She wouldn't trust him as far as she could throw him!

But you aren't in love with Mitch Patrick, jeered a small voice inside her. Of course she wasn't in love with him. She despised his type—arrogant, physical, conceited. It was laughable, absolutely laughable. Are you sure you're not protesting too much? asked that same voice.

Her memory provided her with a replay of their electrifying embrace on the island the night before, and she cringed inwardly. Oh, how easily he had coerced her into responsiveness, forcing away all her sense of duty to Jonathan and to herself as though it had never existed. And she'd allowed him to do it. That was the ultimate degradation.

She hadn't fought him an inch of the way. In fact, it was quite the opposite. Ashleigh burned with self-disgust. And she didn't even have the excuse that she loved him, did she? A funny little pain niggled in the pit of her stomach. No, she wasn't in love with him. She loved Jonathan. And as far as Mitch Patrick was concerned the word love didn't exist. The whole situation could be summed up very truthfully, if not very nicely, in one word. Lust.

CHAPTER SIX

THE long driveway that led to the Denison house swept in a curve through the trees and its first appearance was an extremely spectacular sight. The house appeared to float out from the gentle slope of the hillside, glowing lights in the windows lit up like a small ocean liner. The faint sounds of the sea rolling on the beach below added an auditory backdrop to the scene.

'Isn't it gorgeous, Ash?' breathed Gemma. 'I've never seen anything like it! In the daylight it's like a mountain chalet, all roof angles and open decks. And wait till you see the view of the beach from the living-room!'

'Certainly looks impressive,' Ashleigh agreed, a little taken aback by the opulence of the Denisons.

'I was almost petrified the first time Joel brought me home,' put in Gemma. 'That was on top of being terrified of meeting Joel's father.' She parked the car on the edge of the driveway and as they approached the front door it swung open and Joel ran down the short flight of steps.

'Hi, love!' He kissed Gemma and turned to grin broadly at Ashleigh. 'Do I get a nice sisterly kiss from you, too, Ashleigh?' he teased.

Ashleigh laughed and kissed him lightly on the cheek. 'I think you're going to be in your element in our family of females, Joel Denison!'

'Ryan and Liv came back from the island today,' he told them as he walked them inside, an arm about each of them. 'They'll be calling after dinner, so you'll be meeting the entire family, Ashleigh. They've met Gem,' his smile went to his fiancée, 'and they're thoroughly satisfied with having her as part of the Denison clan. Now, all that's left is for me to make a good impression on the Craigs.'

'You will, Joel,' laughed Ashleigh. 'They'll all be captivated.'

'Sure hope so,' Joel laughed. 'Liv's dying to meet you, Ash. She says she feels she knows you already after acting as go-between throughout your bit of excitement.'

'It was good of her to ring Mother and relieve some of her worry,' said Gemma.

Joel ushered them into the most beautiful living-room Ashleigh had ever seen. Huge anti-glare plate-glass partitions from floor to ceiling dominated the room, and Gemma drew her across the deep-pile carpet to gaze out at the moonlit view of surf and sand.

'Isn't it divine?'

'Beautiful,' Ashleigh agreed inadequately.

'D.J. shouldn't be long. What would you two like to drink?' Joel asked as he walked behind a largish and well-stocked bar. 'Cinzano, Gem?'

Gemma nodded.

'How about you, Ashleigh?'

'I'll have the same, thanks.' Ashleigh stood with her back to the room, her eyes still moving over the beauty of the scene below.

'Beer for me, Joel, if you're playing barman,' said a deep voice that caused Ashleigh to stiffen instinctively before she slowly turned around.

His eyes were on her; she knew they were before she even moved to look at him; and as they gazed across at each other, Ashleigh's skin prickled as though he had physically touched her. The corners of his mouth moved upwards fractionally in a cynical smile, as though he knew quite well how disturbed she was to see him there.

'Hi, Mitch!' Joel's voice cut between them and Mitch turned his gaze away from Ashleigh towards his cousin. 'You don't look any the worse for wear after your adventure, apart from the theatrical patch on your cheek,' he teased. 'Neither does Ashleigh. Any after-effects?' he directed at her as he handed Mitch a glass of frosty beer.

'Absolutely none,' Ashleigh replied firmly, her eyes remaining levelly on Mitch Patrick. She was determined he wasn't going to know the havoc he created within her.

'Where's D.J.?' Mitch turned away and took a sip of his drink.

'Waiting on a phone call,' Joel replied. 'He shouldn't be long.'

'Talking about phone calls, Joel,' Gemma said softly. 'Is it all right if Ashleigh uses your phone to ring Jonathan? She'll reverse the charges.'

'Of course, Ashleigh. Couldn't you reach him this afternoon? Do you want to try now?' Joel asked.

'Oh, no. He won't be back till eight-thirty.' Ashleigh could feel Mitch's eyes on her again. 'But I'd appreciate it if I could ring him after dinner.'

'Sure thing,' said Joel as his father joined them.

D.J. Denison was a tall, rugged man, not carrying an ounce of flesh on his large frame, and he smiled at Ashleigh as Joel made the introductions. 'Glad to meet you, Ashleigh. I can't tell you how pleased I am with Joel's choice of your sister for his wife. Joel tells me you're getting married yourself fairly soon.'

'Yes. In a few weeks.' Ashleigh's eyes flashed over to Mitch and flicked away again, but he'd turned away to set his empty glass on the counter.

'Pity. Seems like we always miss out,' he laughed, his eyes twinkling. 'Hey, Mitch?'

Mitch did look at Ashleigh then and only she caught the mockery in his crooked smile. 'It appears so,' he said ambiguously.

D.J. glanced at his wristwatch. 'Well, shall we go in to dinner?' He held out his arm to Ashleigh with good-natured formality.

They were all seated in the large comfortable chairs in the living-room when Joel's brother and sister-in-law arrived. Ryan and Liv Denison made a striking couple, Ryan so dark, Liv so fair. Ryan was tall and broad-shouldered and, apart from the difference in their colouring, Ryan and Mitch looked more like brothers than Ryan and Joel.

Liv made a beeline for Ashleigh, smiling widely. 'You must be Ashleigh. I'm Liv Denison.' She sat down on the couch next to Ashleigh. 'Well, what an introduction to the Whitsundays you've had.'

'Yes. The type of thing that usually only happens in novels,' Ashleigh smiled back at Liv, liking her immediately.

'And a more romantic hero than Mitch you couldn't find anywhere,' laughed Joel. 'Apart from me, of course, but that's pretty obvious.'

'Ashleigh would have been safer with you, Joel, than with old Casanova Patrick here,' Ryan joined in. 'Simply judging on past form.'

Ashleigh could feel her cheeks beginning to flush and her eyes went to Mitch as he leaned easily on the bar counter. Her heartbeats had accelerated alarmingly as the memories came flooding back. She watched him lazily change his position before answering his cousins' jibes.

'Now I went to great pains to make a good impression on Ashleigh, didn't I?' His eyes laughed into hers. 'If you two aren't careful you'll ruin the whole thing.'

'Oh, I don't think they will, Mitch,' Ashleigh smiled across at him. 'I usually trust in my first impressions, so they'd already been made.'

His smile never faltered, but his eyes narrowed on her making her congratulate herself on one barb going home. The others were all laughing, but Ashleigh knew that her understatement had not been lost on Mitch. And he said she was transparent! All she needed to do was attack him in his oversized ego and she could score a direct hit.

'Where are the twins tonight?' Joel was asking his sister-in-law.

'Spending a few days with the Costellos,' Liv replied, and turned to Ashleigh. 'The Costellos are good friends of ours and their two children, Dino and Sophy, have been holidaying with us on the island. Now Luke and Mellie are staying with Dino and Sophy. It gives Maria and me a few days' break. And to tell you the truth, I'm beginning to need it, with the baby due in about eight weeks.'

'You're feeling quite well, aren't you, Liv?' asked D.J., frowning.

'Oh, yes, I'm fine. Just get a little tired keeping up with the twins,' she smiled back.

'They're both looking forward to the new arrival,' said Joel. 'Luke took me confidentially aside to tell me although he didn't really mind he'd prefer a brother, and Mellie confided that she'd rather have a sister.'

'Well, someone's going to be disappointed,' laughed D.J. 'Unless you make it another set of twins, Liv!'

'Have a bit of pity, D.J.,' groaned Ryan, putting his arm around his wife's shoulders. 'One will be quite adequate, thanks!'

'I seem to remember something being mentioned about triplets some time ago,' Liv laughed up at her husband, and a silent message passed between them both.

That's the way it should be between loving married couples, Ashleigh thought, and her eyes moved involuntarily across to Mitch. He was smiling faintly at Liv and Ryan, then his eyes found hers, and the moment before the cynical mask fell down, when his eyes held a softness she hadn't seen in them before, Ashleigh's breath caught somewhere in her throat and her heart flipped over. If only . . .

Hastily she looked away, hoping she hadn't had any of her thoughts written on her face. If only things could have been different between herself and Mitch! If he wasn't so . . . There's no future in those kind of wishes, she told herself angrily. Besides, Mitch Patrick was the last person she needed to become involved with, he just wasn't the constant type. He was the exact opposite of Jonathan.

Jonathan! She looked quickly at her wristwatch. Eight-thirty-five. She was five minutes late already. Under cover of the conversation she asked Joel if she might be excused to use the phone.

'Of course, Ashleigh,' he replied immediately. 'Use the one in the study—first door through the hall there on your left. Think you'll be able to find it, or shall I come with you?'

'No, thanks, I'll manage, Joel,' Ashleigh excused herself.

'I'll show you the way,' Mitch had his hand under her elbow and they were in the hall before Ashleigh could protest.

'I'm sure I can find my own way, thank you,' she said bitingly, and reached out for the doorknob of the first room on the left.

His hand was there before hers and he swung the door inwards with a short laugh. 'But you might have got lost. This is such a big house, and after last night I kind of find myself responsible for you, Ashleigh.'

'There's absolutely no need for you to feel anything for me, Mr Patrick.' Ashleigh stepped into the large study, turning to close the door after her.

'Oh, but I do,' he replied, his large frame lounging against the door frame. 'Miss Craig,' he added with smiling mockery. 'Come now, Ashleigh, surely we know each other well enough to use christian names? You didn't seem to have any qualms about calling me Mitch last night. Or this morning.'

Ashleigh turned away from him, forcing her anger down. 'You've done your duty, Mr Patrick. You've led me safely to the telephone.' She walked across to the desk and picked up the receiver. 'And now would you kindly have the good manners to let me have some privacy while I make my call.'

She dialled the operator and her call was answered immediately. 'May I make a reverse charge call to Mr Jonathan Randall?' She gave the number and her name, listening while the operator spoke to Jonathan and her call was switched through.

'Ashleigh? What's been happening up there?' Jonathan's voice came clearly over the line.

'Nothing really. Didn't Mother tell you about it?' she asked, feeling like a schoolgirl standing before the teacher reporting on a misdemeanour.

'Yes, yes—she said something about you having to land on a beach in a storm or some such,' Jonathan replied a trifle shortly. 'You know your mother, I could barely piece the story together.'

'Mother was understandably upset,' said Ashleigh, feeling irritated at his criticism.

'Yes, well, I suppose she was. What did happen, then? I've still not been told the details.'

'I was . . . I was sightseeing over the Reef in a small plane and a storm blew up, so we had to land on the beach of a small island and the plane tipped up, so we were stranded until help arrived.' Ashleigh's voice kept catching in her throat.

'For heaven's sake, Ashleigh, what possessed you to go up in a small plane? I thought you couldn't bear the things.'

'I . . . well, Gemma and Joel, they thought I should see a bit of the islands and the Reef before I came back to Brisbane, so they suggested the plane,' Ashleigh finished rather lamely.

'I hope no one else was injured. How many of you were there in the plane?'

'Oh, just . . . just two. Myself and the pilot. It was only a two-seater. Luckily the pilot was very competent. He knew the area and he remembered the island. There was a shelter, so we were relatively dry while we sat the storm out.' Ashleigh stopped herself fiddling nervously with the phone cord.

'Ashleigh, I hope you realise just how lucky you've been. In the hands of an inexperienced pilot you could have been killed. I'd like to personally express my gratitude to the fellow, but as I can't would you do it for me?'

'Of course.'

'How long were you stranded?' Jonathan asked.

Ashleigh had been dreading this question and now that it had been asked she knew she could only be truthful about it. 'About . . . we were on the island about seventeen hours all told. By the time the storm had passed it was dark, so we had to stay put. Then Joel arrived in his plane and between them Joel and Mitch had us back before lunch.'

'You and the pilot were on the island all night?'

'Yes. There was nothing we could do about it,' she said defensively.

'I see. Well, at least you're safe. Now what time will you be back tomorrow? I should be able to collect you.'

'I can't get back tomorrow, Jonathan. There wasn't a seat. It will have to be Monday.'

'Monday? Ashleigh, I postponed going to Sydney until Monday so I could collect you from the airport tomorrow. Are you absolutely certain you can't get an earlier flight?'

Ashleigh could imagine the frown on Jonathan's face. 'No, I'm sorry. There's no way I can get back, not even by bus.'

'I knew something like this would happen! I told you your trip up there was unnecessary and now you're virtually stranded.' He sighed heavily. 'It's most in-convenient.'

'I'm sorry if I've upset your arrangements, Jonathan,' Ashleigh said clippedly, feeling her anger rising, 'but there's nothing I can do about it. Can you rearrange your trip to Sydney?'

'I may be able to,' he replied with ill grace.

'Is it a new client?' she asked.

'Well, no, not exactly.' Jonathan's voice sounded uncharacteristically vague. 'Actually, it's June Sanders. You remember her husband passed away a few months ago?'

'Oh, yes. They owned a chain of hardware stores, didn't they?'

'Yes. There were a couple of branches in Sydney as well and as June is a little unsure of herself business-wise she's asked me to advise her.'

'Oh. Look, Jon, I'm sorry this has thrown your appointments into disorder. Don't worry about picking me up from the airport—Adrie or Vicki can do that. And I'll see you when you get back from Sydney.'

'I'll see what can be arranged, Ashleigh. Phone me if you manage to change your flight. I'll say goodbye, then.'

'Jonathan?' Ashleigh's fingers were twisting the phone cord again.

'Yes?'

'Jon, I . . . I've missed you.'

There was a slight pause. Yes. Well, I've missed you, too. That goes without saying, doesn't it?'

'I suppose so. Goodbye, Jonathan.'

'Goodbye, my dear.'

Ashleigh replaced the receiver and stood looking down at it, feeling dissatisfied. She ran her fingers through her short fair hair, lifting it out from her head, realising she was hot and tense. Somehow, her call hadn't gone as she had expected it would, and she felt flat, emotionally disorientated. And her niggling feeling of disquiet had not been banished at all. Absently she turned back to the door.

Her eyes flew open when they encountered Mitch Patrick leaning easily in the doorway where she'd left him. He must have been there all the time. Typical of his ill manners! When she'd pointedly asked him to leave her.

'I thought I'd asked you to go,' Ashleigh blazed at him, 'but I might have known it would be too much to expect of anyone as insensitive and uncouth as you are!'

'Insensitive and uncouth? Mmm, you haven't used those two words on me before. I wonder how many more you'll be able to find,' he smiled, folding his arms across his broad chest.

'I suppose you make a habit of listening to other people's private conversations?'

He shrugged and pushed himself upright, putting his hands on his hips. 'I thought you might need me to talk to good old Jonathan, assure him that I'd,' he paused, 'looked after you.'

'Well, as you obviously heard, I didn't need you to say anything. Jonathan was simply pleased to be re-assured that I was all right.' Ashleigh stood before him, her eyes flashing. 'I told you he was level-headed and mature.'

'So you did.' He watched her through half-closed lids. 'He didn't mind you sharing your bed with me last night?'

'We didn't share a bed, Mr Patrick—and no, Jonathan didn't mind that we were on the island alone. I told you he trusted me.' Ashleigh irrationally half wished that Jonathan had shown some little sign that he was jealous. But of course Jonathan wasn't that type of person. The fact that they were engaged to be married would preclude any petty feelings of jealousy.

'But we know he can't trust you, don't we, Ash?' Mitch had taken a slow step forward and stood closer to her.

Ashleigh refused to allow him to see the effect his nearness had on her and she valiantly stood her ground.

'Well, Ashleigh? Nothing to say?' His smile mocked.

'What do you want me to say, Mr Patrick?' She strove to hold on to the shreds of her dignity. 'That I lost my head for a moment and almost made the biggest mistake of my life? That the tension of the landing, the aftermath of the drama, the romance of the situation got the better of me?' Her chin rose. 'Because that's all it was. Any presentable male would have done at that moment, I suspect you know that. And I would have hated myself and you afterwards.'

There were a few seconds' silence between them and Ashleigh looked down at her hands. 'I guess I haven't thanked you for . . . for not taking advantage of me when . . . when you could have, but,' she looked up at him defiantly, 'well, now I am thanking you. But I refuse to keep doing it every moment we're together.'

'Your thanks is the last thing I want,' he said shortly, frowning with irritation.

'Then what is it you do want?' Ashleigh asked him softly, her heart beating crazily.

'I'm damned if I know,' he replied almost to himself, running his hand distractedly through his fair hair. 'All I know is that you seem to bring out the worst in me, Ashleigh. Even now. All I really want to do is . . .' He stopped and turned away, leaning on one hand on the door jamb.

'Is what?' She took an involuntary step after him,

knowing she was playing with fire but not being able to stop herself.

Mitch turned his head to look at her, his eyes burning, settling with ardent intensity on the trembling fullness of her lips. 'God, Ashleigh, do you know what you're inviting? You must know—you're not that naïve.' As he spoke he swung back to her, his hands reaching out, drawing her against him, his lips kissing her eyes, the tip of her nose, and at last finding her lips.

Beneath her fingers on his chest Ashleigh faintly registered that his heart was thumping in unison with her own as their bodies moulded together. The soft light cotton of his knit shirt was as sensuous to her fingers as smooth satin and the gabardine of his slacks, moulding the firm muscles of his thighs, barely disguised the heat of aroused senses that seared through the thin crêpe of her dress.

Mitch's hands moved slowly over her hips holding her against him, went to the sensitive hollow of her backbone, carrying her along on waves of disorientating desire. As his lips teased her earlobe she softly moaned his name and he pulled her incredibly closer.

'Say it again, Ashleigh,' he murmured thickly in her ear. 'Say my name again.'

'Oh, Mitch. Please!' Ashleigh tried to push him away, knowing that was the last thing she wanted to do.

'Please what?' His lips found the pulse throbbing at the base of her throat.

'Mitch, we shouldn't . . .' One of his hands moved to cup the fullness of her breast and the words died on her lips as his mouth claimed hers again, reaching down into her very soul.

Eventually Mitch raised his head to look down at her and shook his head slowly, his hands absently playing over her upper arms. 'Ashleigh, I've never wanted anyone as much as I want you.' He ran one finger gently along her cheek, over the fullness of her lips still throbbing from his kisses. His eyes watched her. 'Come back with me tonight,' he said softly, his voice low and sensuous. 'To my place.'

A tiny pain began jabbing in the region of her heart and grew until she had to close her eyes. 'No,' she replied simply.

'Just no.' His finger insinuated itself between her lips, retreated to her earlobe, his hand cupping the curve of her jaw.

Ashleigh nodded.

'Why?'

She shook her head, not opening her eyes, not wanting her resolution to be swayed by the passion she knew would be burning in the blue depths of his.

'Because of Jonathan?' he asked expressionlessly.

'No.' She recognised the honesty in that statement and spoke with a little more conviction. 'No, not because of Jonathan. Because of myself.'

'Ashleigh, don't try to tell me you don't want me as much as I want you? Because I won't believe it.' His hand caressed her shoulder with knowing ease and she shivered involuntarily. 'You don't even believe that yourself.'

'I'm . . . I'm not denying it. I do find you,' Ashleigh took a steady breath, 'physically attractive—I can't deny that.'

'Then why? And for God's sake look at me!' He lifted her chin and her eyes looked into his.

'I can't just have an affair with you, Mitch,' she said

at last, and he released her to pace across the carpet, his hand running through his hair again, the muscles of his shoulders and back outlined beneath the soft material of his shirt.

'You've got me where you want me, Ashleigh, eating out of your hand,' he said quietly. 'When I'm with you I can't keep my own hands off you.'

'I'm sorry. I told you I can't . . . Mitch, if I'd—well, slept around as seems to be the fashion these days it might be easier to do, but I . . . It's not me,' she finished lamely.

'What is you, then, Ashleigh?' He turned around, aggression in every angle of his body. 'No, let me guess. The white dress, the flowers, the rings, till death us do part, and a piece of paper that gets filed in with the house mortgage and the children's birth certificates.' His tone had sharpened cynically.

'It's what some women need. Maybe not as many as there used to be, but it seems to work out for most people,' she said softly. 'I think it means something to me.'

'Well, I'm not most people. You've picked the wrong guy, Ashleigh. I don't need those kind of promises of forever. Forever doesn't mean what it used to mean. It's lost a lot of its conviction. As I see it, it's almost obsolete.'

'What made you so cynical, Mitch? Or should I say who?' she asked him, feeling emotionally numb.

He gave a harsh laugh then. 'It would have to be a woman, wouldn't it? Oh, no, don't colour me with a broken heart. A broken heart's very often a romantic way of saying wounded pride or bruised ego.'

Ashleigh shook her head, a dull ache beginning to thaw the numbness inside her.

'Ashleigh, I'm not going to beg for your favours,' he said harshly.

Her anger rose then, her eyes flashing luminous bright blue. 'I didn't ask you to,' she bit out.

Mitch laughed mirthlessly and shook his head. 'You know, you don't have to search far for proof of what I say. Look at yourself, at that ring you're wearing. Doesn't that mean some kind of forever to you and good old Jonathan? Or should I say, *didn't* it mean forever?'

'Why, you . . .'

'I rest my case, Ashleigh.' He spread his hands, that same cynical smile on his face.

'You're contemptible! I wonder if you realise just how juvenile you sound. You're like a child who can't have what he wants. It won't surprise me in the least if you now go off in a fit of the sulks.' Her lip curled.

He took a step towards her and she retreated backwards until she came up against the desk. 'Aren't you afraid I might childishly want to smash the toy that's denied me?' he asked with ominous quietness.

'Keep away from me!' Ashleigh cried, leaning over the desk away from him as he moved closer.

His hands pulled her savagely against him, his lips punishing her, bruising the softness of her mouth, and she pushed ineffectually against him. When Mitch eventually surrendered her lips they were both breathing heavily and he smiled crookedly, his hands still holding her against the hardness of his body.

'As I said, you bring out the worst in me, Ash.' His voice was low and thick. 'Perhaps it might be best if you make haste for home and the safety of good old Jonathan who trusts and respects you.'

'Mitch, I . . . you don't mean that.' The words were

out before Ashleigh could stop herself voicing them.

'Don't I? I think I do.'

Ashleigh cringed inside at the rejection in his expressionless words.

'Don't look to me for your knight in shining armour. I'm just a man with a man's needs and an honest and realistic outlook on life.'

'A man's needs?' Ashleigh's temper rose. 'You know, you are one hell of a selfish swine! You talk about your needs and that's where it ends. What about mine? And as for being honest and realistic, that's the last thing you are. If you were honest you'd admit that what you need is someone who's prepared to be a body whenever you feel the urge. Someone who'll agree that the world's a terribly insecure place and therefore it's not worth making any long-range plans for it.' Ashleigh gulped a ragged breath. 'Well, that's all just plain excuses, manufactured to quell your conscience. You're a coward, Mitch, an emotional coward!'

His fingers tightened on her arms until she had to bite her lip against the pain.

'If you were a man I'd lay you out for that,' he told her, his face tensed in anger.

'Why discriminate over a little thing like that?' Ashleigh goaded him, wanting to hit out at him.

'Ashleigh, take care! I'm not some wishy-washy Goody Two-Shoes you can manipulate any way you like.'

His words were clipped, and suddenly all the fight seemed to drain out of her.

'Oh, what's the use, Mitch? We're on different wavelengths. I just can't be what you want me to be. You'll have to accept that.' And so will I, she added to herself.

'Ashleigh?' His biting hold had changed to a caress.

A cough at the door distracted them both, and as Joel stepped into the study Mitch slowly dropped his hands, a frown darkening his brow as he turned towards his cousin. 'What do you want, Joel?' he asked without attempting to conceal his displeasure at the interruption, a fact that seemed to amuse Joel even more.

'I'm the search party,' he grinned, looking from one to the other. 'I put them off as long as I could, but everyone was sure you'd both lost your way, so I was pressured into taking the plunge.'

'Well, you've found us.' Mitch moved towards the door, leaving Ashleigh to follow.

'So I have. Hope I didn't interrupt anything,' Joel teased. Even from where she stood behind him Ashleigh felt the shock waves from the look Mitch bestowed on his cousin and as he strode into the hall Ashleigh caught his barely civil words.

'Go to hell, Joel!'

Joel laughed aloud then, turning to wait for Ashleigh to precede him out of the study. 'Something tells me the tiger has had his fur ruffled!'

Ashleigh dropped her eyes, her cheeks pink.

'It won't kill him, Ash. In fact, it will do him the world of good,' chuckled Joel. 'Don't get me wrong, I feel for Mitch as though he was my brother, but I'm afraid I don't see eye to eye with him on one or two subjects.'

'Neither do I,' Ashleigh said quietly, but with feeling nonetheless, as they re-entered the living-room.

'Did you get through to Jonathan?' asked Gemma, her eyes taking in her sister's flushed face.

'Yes. We . . . we had a long chat,' Ashleigh replied,

feeling her colour deepen even further.

Mitch was standing by the bar pouring himself a drink and made no comment even though Ashleigh half expected him to contradict her statement.

'Joel and Ryan have come up with a great idea, Ashleigh,' said Gemma. 'Did Joel tell you?'

'No. What idea was that?' Ashleigh dragged her mind away from Mitch's uncompromising back.

'We could all go sailing at the weekend. I mean, if you're not going home until Monday we can take you to see Craven Island. What do you think, Ash?' Gemma beamed enthusiastically.

'Oh, sounds like fun,' Ashleigh replied, hoping Mitch would be tied up with his aeroplane.

'It will be,' laughed Liv. 'Ryan suggests we leave early Saturday morning and we can spend the night on the island and sail back Sunday afternoon. What about you, Mitch? Are you free this weekend?'

'Unfortunately I think we've got bookings on Saturday and Sunday,' he replied noncommittally.

'That's no worry, mate,' put in Joel. 'Get Jim to do this weekend for you. You're always taking his shift when he wants time off.'

'I suppose I could,' Mitch didn't sound enthusiastic, 'if he's willing.'

'Right, that's settled,' said Ryan. 'I'll check the tides and let you know what time to be down at the wharf.'

'Just wait till we're cutting through the water, Ashleigh,' smiled Liv, 'you'll be ecstatic!'

Ashleigh's eyes crossed to Mitch. 'I'm sure I'll love it,' she said, hoping the thought of Mitch joining their weekend wouldn't take the conviction out of her voice. But maybe he wouldn't come along.

The night wore on, and had it not been for the tension that existed between herself and Mitch Ashleigh would have enjoyed it, for she liked Joel and his family very much. Watching Gemma filled her with happiness for her sister. In the months since she had left home Gemma had found herself. She now joined in conversations, albeit quietly, and seemed to find no hardship in expressing her views. In the centre of the Craig menagerie she had rarely made her presence felt.

'Can you two drop Mitch off at his flat?' Joel's words brought Ashleigh back to earth with a thud. 'He's leaving the four-wheel-drive for me to pick him up in the morning.'

'Of course. Are you ready to go, Mitch?' Gemma asked, shooting a quick glance at Ashleigh.

'Whenever you are.'

'All right. Thanks for the lovely evening.' Gemma put her hand into Joel's as they walked to the door.

'We might head off, too,' said Ryan. 'Nice meeting you, Ashleigh. We'll see you all on Saturday bright and early.'

'Do you want to drive as far as your flat, Mitch?' Gemma asked him nervously as they reached the car.

'No, thanks, Gemma.' Mitch smiled at her. 'I have every faith in your driving. Besides, I'm sure Ashleigh would call me a male chauvinist if I didn't.' His smile faded as he turned to hold the front door open for Ashleigh to climb into the passenger seat.

'Oh, Mitch, I'm sure Ashleigh wouldn't think that,' Gemma said quickly. 'Would you, Ash?'

'Of course I wouldn't.' Ashleigh's tone belied her words and she smiled sweetly at Mitch as she took her seat.

The journey to Mitch's flat was accomplished in silence. Gemma made an attempt to coax the other two into conversation, but gave up when both Ashleigh and Mitch were obviously loath to talk.

'Did you leave the light on in your flat when you came out?' asked Gemma as she pulled into the curb in front of a single-storey block of units.

'No.' Mitch was out of the car almost before it stopped. 'You two stay put.'

He was halfway across the small expanse of lawn when the door of the flat was opened and a slight figure raced with the shaft of light over the grass to hurl itself at Mitch's approaching figure. Ashleigh sprang out of the car to go to his assistance when she realised that far from being attacked Mitch was being very thoroughly kissed. Trembling, Ashleigh stopped as suddenly as she had started, and as Mitch's arms went around the other figure her heart twisted painfully.

Gemma had left the car and was standing beside Ashleigh. Mitch's hands went up and firmly removed the thin arms from around his neck before stepping back, his eyes seemingly fixed on the girl. For now Ashleigh could make out the neat figure clad in tight figure-hugging jeans and T-shirt and the cascade of long dark curls.

'Mitch darling, I've been waiting ages for you!' Her voice was soft and petulant. 'Aren't you surprised to see me?'

'Just what are you doing here, Megan?'

Ashleigh could feel sorry for the girl at the tone Mitch used. That he was not overjoyed to see the girl was so blatantly obvious, and it crossed Ashleigh's mind that this could be herself after a few weeks, maybe a few months. One of Mitch Patrick's cast-offs. Her anger blazed towards him and she swung back to the car just as Mitch turned around to face them.

'Is everything all right, Mitch?' Gemma asked, her hands clasped together, not knowing whether to stand her ground or follow Ashleigh back to the car.

'Yes. This is Megan Astill, a cousin of mine. Megan, meet Gemma Craig, Joel's fiancée, and her sister Ashleigh. Megan, as usual, has omitted to inform me of her pending arrival,' he added drily.

'Have I come at an inconvenient time, darling?' The girl looked up at him through her lashes. 'And I'm really a very distant cousin numerous times removed, thank goodness.' Her eyes turned speculatively over the other two girls.

'Hello, Megan.' Gemma's eyes went to Ashleigh as she stood by the open door of the car. 'I . . . I guess we should be going, shouldn't we, Ash? We'll . . . we'll see you on Saturday, Mitch. Goodnight.'

'Goodnight, Gem. Ashleigh.' He nodded in Ashleigh's direction, his features in shadow with the light behind him.

Ashleigh didn't say a word. She knew she had made the right decision. What Mitch Patrick asked of her was impossible . . . His terms were too high. When she went back to Brisbane she would be able to put him behind her, and after a while even this pain inside her would begin to dull.

CHAPTER SEVEN

'Do you suppose she's his girl-friend, Ashleigh?' Gemma asked as they drove away. 'She seemed awfully young. Although it was a bit hard to see in the semi-darkness.'

'I've no idea, but it wouldn't surprise me in the least,' Ashleigh fixed her interest on the lights in the houses and businesses they passed.

'I didn't think he was very pleased to see her, did you? I mean, he was very brusque with her, wasn't he?'

'Perhaps he'd got what he wanted and he'd lost interest in her,' Ashleigh said flatly.

'Ashleigh!' Gemma was shocked. 'That's a bit steep, isn't it? I don't think Mitch is that bad. Maybe she is his cousin, from up north—that's where he comes from. His family have a dairy property somewhere on the Atherton Tableland.'

'Pity he hadn't stayed there.' Ashleigh couldn't keep the bitterness out of her voice.

'Ash, what's the matter? I've never seen you like this before. Usually you haven't got an unkind word to say about anyone.' Gemma frowned.

'Don't worry about it, love.' Ashleigh sighed. 'Mitch Patrick just rubs me the wrong way, that's all.'

'Did he . . . well . . . did he make a pass at you?'

Ashleigh gave a short laugh. 'I think Mitch Patrick is conditioned to making a pass at anyone female between the ages of six and sixty. It's part of his nature.'

'Oh, Ashleigh,' Gemma sighed, 'perhaps you're right. I guess I'm pretty naïve about men. But I've always felt sort of sorry for him.'

'Sorry for him?' Ashleigh repeated incredulously. 'For heaven's sake, why?'

'I don't know,' Gemma shrugged. 'He just seems a bit lonely, I guess. Joel says he doesn't really get on with his family.'

'That I can understand. But as to the lonely bit, I should imagine he doesn't go without a certain type of company.' Ashleigh said drily.

'Well, if that's true then it's even sadder,' remarked Gemma quietly. 'He must get awfully bored.'

Ashleigh made no comment on that and they drove on to the flat in silence.

Joel collected them just before daybreak on Saturday morning. Of Mitch they had seen nothing since Wednesday evening and Ashleigh felt herself fighting fluctuating feelings. One minute she tingled with anticipation and then she fell to earth with a thud, reminding herself just how selfish and despicable Mitch Patrick really was.

The evening before Joel had collected Gemma's car from the panel-beaters for her and then stayed to dinner. Neither Ashleigh nor Gemma brought Mitch's name into the conversation and they were sitting over their coffee before Joel mentioned him.

'I believe Mitch introduced you to Megan the other night,' he said, his eyes on Ashleigh's face.

'Yes, he did,' replied Gemma. 'She . . . I think he was surprised to see her. He said he didn't know she was coming.'

'He never does know with Megan.' Joel's voice held mild disapproval.

'Is she his girl-friend?' asked Gemma. 'I can't say I've heard either of you mention her before.'

'They've known each other since they were children. Their families live close by each other and I think both sets of parents expected Mitch and Megan to make a couple,' explained Joel.

'And I suppose he didn't want to do what was expected of him,' remarked Ashleigh.

'I don't really know what Mitch thinks about that, but it seems Megan can't decide which brother she prefers, Mitch or Matt.'

'Matt's his twin brother, isn't he? How does he feel about it all?' asked Gemma.

'Don't know,' Joel shrugged. 'Matt's a quiet sort of guy. If he's upset about it he keeps it to himself. Anyway, looks like she'll be staying with Mitch for a while.' He glanced across at Ashleigh and added quickly, 'She's taken the flat next door to his. The tenants are away for a couple of months, so that fits in pretty well.'

After that the conversation turned to more comfortable topics, and now here they were on their way down to the wharf for a weekend of sailing.

Most people would give their eye teeth for an opportunity to spend time sailing on a large yacht through the Whitsunday Islands, Ashleigh mused, and on any other occasion she knew she would have been ecstatic about it, too. But with Mitch Patrick making up the party—well, that was something else again. She had to admit that it was herself she was most angry with, angry at her own weakness, but she still recognised that Mitch Patrick was the instigator of all her anger, her disquieting soul-searching. Yet she couldn't suppress a spurt of anticipation that she would be seeing him again.

Ryan's yacht undulated gently beside the wharf, and Ashleigh experienced a quiver of delight at its beauty. Mitch Patrick or no Mitch Patrick, she was glad she had come along, and she began to look forward to the moment when they would be cutting through the water. Liv and Ryan were on the deck and both waved a greeting.

'Ah, here comes the crew.' Ryan sprang ashore and relieved Ashleigh of her overnight case.

'Hi!' called Liv. 'Glad to see you remembered to bring your party gear,' she said as Ashleigh carefully carried their dresses on board. 'Ryan will take them below.' She passed the hangers to her husband. 'We'll have dinner at the restaurant tonight. Wasn't that a good idea of mine?' she beamed. 'And we can dance afterwards. Or at least I'll watch you all dancing.' She pulled a face. 'No disco for me for a while!'

'I should think not,' Joel admonished her. 'And you be jolly careful tripping around the decks.'

'I've been trying to tell her that for months,' said Ryan, rejoining them. 'But you know Liv. It's a wonder I haven't turned grey-haired overnight with worry.'

'Don't despair, darling. Grey hair is most distinguished.' Liv slid her arm around his waist and reached up to kiss him lightly on the cheek. 'You'll be even more attractive than you are now.'

Ryan grinned broadly and winked at Ashleigh and Gemma. 'You can see why I keep her around. Does wonders for my ego!' He pulled her against him and kissed the tip of her nose.

Joel smiled indulgently at his brother and sister-in-law. 'It's absolutely disgusting the way you married people carry on,' he teased them. 'Never see us single folk doing that, do you, girls?' he appealed to Gemma and Ashleigh, and they all laughed.

'Did Mitch change his mind about coming?' asked Gemma.

'Not as far as I know.' Ryan glanced at his watch. 'He is a bit late. That's not like him.'

'Isn't Megan coming with him?' put in Liv.

'Oh.' Ryan and Joel looked at each other.

'That explains everything,' said Joel.

'Well, we may as well find ourselves a comfortable seat,' said Liv. 'Come on, we'll get out of the way and settle down ready to watch the men at work.' She sighed as she made herself comfortable. 'Poor Mitch! I hope Megan doesn't hold him up for too long.'

'Is she a bit of a slowcoach?' asked Gemma.

'You could say that,' replied Liv drily, and frowned slightly. 'I hope she doesn't . . .' She stopped and seemed to shake off whatever she was thinking. Forcing a smile, she made a sweeping gesture at the yacht. 'Well, enough of that. What do you think of *Midnight Blue*? Isn't she a beauty?'

'Certainly is.' Ashleigh dragged her own thoughts into order, trying desperately to convince herself that she was not keyed up waiting for Mitch Patrick to put in an appearance.

'Aren't the twins coming with us?' Gemma was asking.

'No. They're still with the Costellos. Mike and Maria are taking them on a picnic this afternoon, so they decided to forgo the sailing in favour of the picnic. It sounded as though the entire Costello clan were going along, so I can imagine the fun they're going to have,' she laughed.

'Here comes Mitch and Megan now.' Joel's voice

drew their attention to the couple approaching the yacht.

Mitch Patrick's long tanned legs strode purposefully across the wharf, his muscular arms carrying two large and one small suitcase without any apparent stress. Behind him came the slight figure of Megan Astill, almost running to keep up with his seemingly effortless strides. However, he did turn back to help the girl up the gangway on to the deck.

'We'd nearly given you up for lost,' remarked Joel as he helped Ryan lash the gangway on to the deck.

'I'm afraid that was my fault, Joel.' Megan put her small hand on to Joel's arm. 'I'm such a sleepyhead in the mornings. Mitch had quite a job waking me up, didn't you, darling? I think he was about to resort to a glass of cold water!'

Mitch made no comment and disappeared below deck with the cases, while Ashleigh kept her eyes on the deck at her feet, trying to ignore the spurt of jealousy that clutched at her as she imagined Mitch and Megan together.

'Why not join the girls, Megan,' Ryan put in, 'and we'll see about getting underway.'

'Hello, Megan.' Liv addressed the other girl. 'You've met Ashleigh and Gemma, haven't you?'

'Yes—the night I arrived.' The smile Megan turned on them appeared a trifle forced.

Now that Ashleigh could study the other girl in daylight she could see that Megan Astill was not as young as they had at first thought. Her figure was perfection itself, neat and trim, and although her make-up was flawless it couldn't totally disguise the lines around her eyes and mouth.

'I think Mitch is a little out of sorts this morning,'

said Gemma as they watched him join Joel and Ryan at the wheel.

'He'll get over it,' remarked Megan offhandedly. 'He always does if I flatter him a bit.' She stood up and walked along the deck to where the three men stood.

Ryan was at the wheel as they motored out of the harbour, while Joel and Mitch stood by ready to raise the sails when they reached the open water. Megan slid an arm about Mitch's waist, saying something softly to him.

'She's very sure of herself, isn't she?' said Gemma to Ashleigh and Liv.

'Maybe she's just sure of him,' remarked Ashleigh flatly, looking away from the closeness of those two figures.

'Don't let Megan fool you, Ashleigh. I can't say how she thinks things stand between Mitch and herself, but Ryan says as far as Mitch is concerned Megan is his brother Matt's girl-friend,' said Liv, her eyes going to Ashleigh expressively, and, a little embarrassed, Ashleigh looked away.

'Oh. That's probably why he didn't seem very pleased to see her the other night. He was terribly short with her,' Gemma all but shuddered. 'I would have died if he'd treated me like that!'

Liv laughed softly. 'Yes, Mitch is a lot like Ryan, rather formidable in his anger. You've no worries in that regard with Joel, Gem. He's a real softie.'

Gemma smiled shyly. 'Joel is pretty wonderful.'

Liv laughed outright. 'I'd have to agree with you there. What do you think of Gem's fiancé, Ashleigh?'

'I think he's wonderful, too,' Ashleigh smiled. 'I don't think Gemma could have asked for anyone nicer.'

'And vice versa,' laughed Liv. 'Now Mitch,' her eyes went to Ashleigh, 'Mitch is a very different kettle of fish.'

'That's the understatement of the year,' Ashleigh remarked, very nearly under her breath, glancing up in time to see a speculative glint in Liv's eyes. 'Tell me about Craven Island,' she added quickly, settling on the first subject that came into her mind that would steer the conversation away from Mitch Patrick and Megan Astill. And Ashleigh didn't care whose girl-friend she professed to be, she told herself firmly, as Liv gave tham a short description of the island resort.

The throb of the engines died and Ashleigh turned to watch as Mitch and Joel raised the sails. As the wind caught and filled the canvas the yacht seemed to lift itself out of the water and begin its race across the ocean's surface, the rigging rattling in the breeze joyously crying encouragement.

'Look at all those strong muscles flexing!' Megan's high voice brought Ashleigh's unconscious gaze away from Mitch's tall figure, tanned body glistening in the bright sunlight.

'Yes. Men at work—a satisfying sight,' laughed Liv.

'Ashleigh can't keep her eyes off them.' Megan's smile didn't reach her dark eyes.

'I'll get a photo of them!' Gemma exclaimed, lifting her camera out of her bag and focusing it on Joel and Mitch as they worked in unison.

'Ain't love grand?' drawled Megan. 'I'll bet she's taken rolls of film of Joel.'

'Not rolls exactly, but I have taken quite a few.' Gemma sat down, her cheeks pink.

Hard brown eyes settled contemplatively on Gemma, and Ashleigh shifted uncomfortably in her seat, feeling her dislike of Megan Astill rise in her again.

'You know, when I heard that Joel was engaged you could have knocked me down with a feather,' said Megan. 'I was sure he was a confirmed bachelor. In fact I would have put my money on it.'

'That was before he met Gem,' Liv put in, smiling gently at the younger girl.

'Yes, but you know what I mean, Liv. Or you should.' The dark eyes went to Liv. Like a snake, thought Ashleigh, cold and bright, ready to strike.

Liv had raised one fine eyebrow questioningly and Megan shrugged.

'Well, it's a known fact that Joel always fancied you, was pining away over you, and frankly, I never thought he'd get over it. He did—er—look after you when Ryan ran out on you. So you'll be able to tell Gemma what a brick he is.'

Ashleigh stiffened as she watched her sister's face fade from dull red to ashen and her eyes went to Liv, whose only outward sign of discomposure was the slight frown on her brow.

'It sounds to me as though you've been avidly listening to ancient gossip, Megan,' Liv remarked evenly, although the tightness of her mouth did suggest anger. 'And apart from being malicious it's all rather boring and old hat. You'd do better to mind your own business.'

'Well! I was only stating the facts,' Megan began.

'No one knows the true facts except the people involved, and as it's nothing to do with you there's no point in your bringing up the subject. Unless you want to upset Gemma or myself,' Liv added, looking levelly at the other girl.

'Oh, really! This conversation's getting so intense—I think I'll go and join the men.' Megan flounced off.

Liv sighed heavily. 'If I thought she was being deliberately malicious . . .' she stopped and turned back to Gemma. 'Don't let what Megan implied upset you, Gem.'

'Oh, I'm not upset, Liv,' Gemma hastened to reassure the other girl. 'I was just taken aback, that's all.'

Ashleigh saw a little colour returning to her sister's face, although her eyes were still slightly troubled as they went to Ashleigh and back to Liv.

'I mean, Joel's so nice and so . . . so handsome,' Gemma continued, 'I know he must have had lots of girl-friends before he met me, but . . .' she stopped.

'But you didn't think I was one of them,' Liv finished. 'I wasn't. There's never been anyone but Ryan for me. Joel and I have always been good friends, since I was a teenager. In fact he was a huge support to me when things weren't going very well for me and I'll always be grateful to him for that. Joel's kind, considerate and sensitive. And I know he loves you,' she added honestly.

Gemma's face broke into a smile. 'I love him, too,' she said softly.

'Well, now we've got that sorted out satisfactorily,' she patted Gemma's hand, 'let's go and brew some coffee.' They stood up. 'No, stay there and relax, Ashleigh. Gem and I will manage.'

Ashleigh sat down again, fighting her own anger. Poor Gemma! How could Megan have been so cruel? If she wasn't spiteful then she was extremely thoughtless—and remembering the coldness of her eyes, Ashleigh was inclined to think it was the former. She turned to watch Megan leaning on the rails alongside Mitch and her anger trebled. They were certainly a good pair, those two!

Standing up, Ashleigh moved to the opposite side of the yacht, putting as much distance as she could between herself and that couple. As she leaned against the safety rails her eyes barely registered the beauty of the blue water washing past the sleek hull of the yacht.

A strand of fair hair whipped across her eyes and she turned her face into the wind, looping her hair behind her ear. The stiff breeze seemed to act as a tranquilliser, soothing her agitated feelings, and for a moment she put it all behind her, relaxing in the enjoyment of the moment. Yes, with her face to the wind as it tugged at the fine tendrils of her hair she could almost convince herself that Mitch Patrick was on some other planet, that he was not on board to discompose her, stir her susceptible senses. When he materialised before her, her bubble burst with a brutal bang.

His eyes were enveloping her again, enmeshing her in the inescapable web of his magnetism. Half closed against the glare, his long lashes bleached silver in the sunlight, those eyes touched each facet of her face, fell lower over the smooth column of her throat, all but physically caressing the full curve of her breasts rising beneath the softness of her terry-towelling T-shirt.

Goosebumps of tingling sensation rose on Ashleigh's suddenly clammy skin and she realised that unconsciously she herself had been drinking in every sensual centimetre of his bronzed body. He had shed his shirt before attending to the sails and her gaze roved over his broad muscular shoulders, her fingers longing to lose themselves in the curling fair hair on his chest, wanting to slide down the firmness of his midriff. His

light shorts hugged his hips and she quickly forced her
eyes back to his face, fighting to quell the wild surges
of her heartbeats, wishing she could convince herself
that he didn't possess the power to arouse her the way
no man had ever done before.

'You look as if you're enjoying yourself,' he said at
last, when she had finally thought the band of taut
tension between them would explode about them.

'I *was*,' she replied with sarcastic emphasis on the
past tense, and his lips tightened, a fact that perversely
brought her no satisfaction whatsoever.

Moving slightly, he leant his hips on the rails, turning his face away from her so that the wind lifted his
fair hair, pulling it back from his face so that she could
study the lines of his profile, the strong forehead, the
almost classical nose, the firm chin and hard square
jaw. And his lips . . . She shivered, telling herself not
to think about his lips, because the next progression
from thinking about his lips was remembering the feel
of them plundering hers.

'Do you think we could cool it for the weekend,
Ashleigh?' he asked quietly. 'I've got enough on my
plate without adding you to it.'

'There's no need to add me to anything to do with
you,' Ashleigh told him.

He made no comment and showed no sign of leaving
her.

'Megan will be looking for you,' she said.

He did turn towards her then, his lips a thin line as
he strove to keep his anger in check. 'Megan is nothing
to me,' he said with ominous quietness.

'She has a strange way of showing it.' Ashleigh raised
one eyebrow. 'But then it may be to your advantage to
keep her on a string.'

'And you sound jealous,' he smiled at her, and Ashleigh took a step away from him at the coldness in his eyes.

'That would be the last thing I'd be,' she told him emphatically.

'Madam, you protest too much.' His finger ran over her hand where she clutched the rail, his hand covering hers, holding it fast when she would have jerked it away. 'Your pulse is racing, Ashleigh,' he said huskily and raised her hand until he could put his lips to that very same place where her heightened awareness of him pounded.

'Let me go!' Ashleigh's senses had reacted to his touch before she could restrain them and her breathing quickened agitatedly.

'You don't mean that.' His voice was liquid silk riding the wind, his eyes burning into hers.

'Isn't one at a time enough for you?' Ashleigh tried to drag her hand from his, only to have his fingers tighten around her wrist, biting cruelly into her flesh.

'What's that supposed to mean?' He pulled her closer to him so that her free hand went to his chest in an effort to fend him off.

'It should be obvious. And you're hurting me!' Her fingers were tingling where they touched him.

'It's not obvious.'

'Oh, forget it and leave me alone.' Ashleigh suddenly wanted done of the whole thing.

'Not till you say what's on your mind. Come on, Ashleigh, don't start something unless you mean to finish it.'

'Go back to Megan,' Ashleigh bit out. 'She at least seems to welcome your so obvious attentions!'

She wasn't even aware that he had moved, for his muscles barely flexed, but suddenly she was leaning precariously over the rails, and the coming sensation of falling had her clutching at the hardness of his arms. For infinite seconds he suspended her there and then she was back on her feet pale and shaken.

'I suppose I should apologise for that,' he said quietly, his jaw tense.

'Would you . . . would you have let me go?' she asked him shakily.

'We'll never know, will we?' he smiled crookedly, then raked his hand through his hair in exasperation. 'If I thought it would give me any peace of mind, yes, I would have tossed you overboard, but somehow I think my peace has been a little more permanently shattered.'

With that he turned and walked away, leaving his enigmatic words spinning inside her, mocking her.

CHAPTER EIGHT

CRAVEN ISLAND grew out of the multi-patterned turquoise water, a green paradise with a fringe of white sand. As they approached the island resort Ashleigh joined the others in watching it grow larger, but although its beauty stirred her aesthetically her mind was wrestling with a far different subject—Mitch Patrick.

Her eyes slid sideways, seeking him out, but his tall body was almost obscured by Ryan. However, she could still see that Megan stood close to him, her arm linked through his. And Mitch didn't appear to be fighting her off either, she thought bitterly.

Less than twenty minutes earlier he had been sending the blood rushing through her body with his lips on her wrist, his eyes implacably caressing her entire body. Absently she massaged the place on the inside of her arm where the pressure of his strong fingers had left dual red marks.

Why couldn't he simply leave her alone? She had made it more than plain that she wasn't interested in having an affair with him. Why couldn't he just take her at her word and look elsewhere for his sordid thrills? She shivered suddenly and wrapped her arms about herself, wishing dispassionately that she had never allowed her family to talk her into leaving Brisbane, so that she would never have set eyes on Mitch Patrick.

When her eyes sought him out again he had moved slightly, leaving her free to drink her fill of him. And the pain that luxury induced left her feeling weak and trembling.

'Is it any wonder they have us caught nicely under their spells?' remarked a quiet voice beside her, and Ashleigh turned startled and unknowingly vulnerable eyes on Liv Denison.

'I . . . I beg your pardon?' she stammered, feeling the heightened colour washing her cheeks.

'The Denison men—they're attractive devils, aren't they?' Liv smiled.

'Oh—yes. Yes, I suppose they are,' Ashleigh agreed.

'That includes Mitch, of course. I always think he's more Denison than anything else.'

'There does appear to be quite a resemblance,' Ashleigh said carefully.

'Falling in love with them can be a trauma in itself.' Liv's eyes rested softly on her tall dark husband.

'I should imagine it would be.' Ashleigh kept all expression from her voice.

'But oh, so worth it,' laughed Liv. 'You can take my word for that, Ashleigh—I'm speaking from experience.'

'I . . .' Ashleigh couldn't find a word to say. She wanted to deny vehemently the implication behind Liv's words. Liv appeared to be under a great misapprehension about Mitch Patrick and herself. There was nothing between them. How on earth had Liv come by that misconception?

'Oh, look! You can see the house now, Ashleigh.' Liv pointed past the sturdy jetty. 'Through the trees there. I love it here on the island—it's so peaceful. You don't have the continuous pressure, the feeling that life's rushing by at a tremendous pace.'

On the jetty stood a fair young man lounging beside

a bright yellow four-wheel-drive. As the yacht nudged the mooring he sprang forward and caught the rope Joel tossed him.

'How are things, Jerry?'

'Fine, Joel. Hi, Mitch. Need a hand with your gear?' The young man sprang effortlessly onto the deck. 'Hi, Boss!' His grin widened as Ryan joined them.

'On time for once, Jerry,' teased Ryan. 'For that you get to drive the ladies up to the house!'

The house was long and low with a covered verandah running its full length; sliding glass doors opening from every room. Brown shutters were folded back from each door and window, adding to the design of the house and obviously having a serviceable value should they be needed during the cyclone season.

As they climbed out of the jeep and mounted the wide steps a middle-aged woman came through the main doors. She was tall and angular, grey hair pulled back into a neat bun, and Liv Denison smiled a greeting.

'Hello, Nance, come and meet everyone. You remember Gemma? Well, this is her sister, Ashleigh Craig. Oh, and I think you know Megan! Ashleigh, this is Nance Williams, a treasure we couldn't do without.'

Ashleigh smiled at the older woman.

'I hope you and your sister don't mind sharing a room, Miss Craig,' said Nance as she led them inside.

'Of course not,' Ashleigh and Gemma spoke together.

'I suppose I'm in my usual room?' remarked Megan. 'If nobody minds I think I'll have a lie down for an hour or so. The movements of the boat make me queasy.'

No one seemed to mind at all.

'Mmm, the water was divine this afternoon, wasn't it?' Gemma turned away from the mirror, her eyes bright. 'Aren't you looking forward to this evening, Ash?'

Absently Ashleigh pulled the brush through her fair hair and had to force her mind back to concentrate on what her sister was saying. 'Yes.'

'You don't sound very enthusiastic,' frowned Gemma. 'Ash, what's the matter? Are you worried about being held up with all your wedding arrangements?'

Ashleigh blinked. Her wedding? Wedding? The word sounded so unfamiliar—and so far away. But she was supposed to be getting married in a matter of weeks. That part of her life at this particular moment seemed to belong to someone else entirely, was almost unreal. And Jonathan—her conscience refused to allow her to think about him.

'Ashleigh?' Gemma's voice broke into her tortured thoughts.

'Hmmm? Oh, I'm sorry, Gem, I was miles away.' She shrugged her shoulders. 'And no, I'm not worried about the wedding arrangements. In fact, I don't think . . . I won't be going through with the wedding now.' There, it had been said. Ashleigh felt only relief that she had at last voiced what had been turning in her mind for some time, although she had been afraid to give the decision rein.

Gemma sat down on the bed beside her sister, her face expressing her shock. 'But, Ashleigh, why?'

'Lots of reasons.' Ashleigh wiped her hand over her forehead. 'I haven't even sorted it out myself yet. But I do know it wouldn't be a very good idea.'

'I can't believe it, Ashleigh! I mean, you and Jonathan have known each other for so long and everyone always thought . . .' Gemma stopped. 'Did you discuss it on the phone the other night? I thought you looked a bit disturbed when you came back.'

Ashleigh shook her head. 'No, I haven't told Jonathan how I feel. I think I should wait till I get back so I . . . we can talk it over properly.'

'Maybe it's just pre-wedding nerves, Ashleigh. Maybe you'll feel better when you see Jonathan again,' Gemma suggested.

'I don't think I will, Gem,' she said flatly.

They were silent for a moment.

'Is it because of Mitch?' Gemma asked quietly.

Ashleigh stood up then and paced across to the dressing table, setting her brush down and picking it up again. 'Of course not! What could he have to do with it? I scarcely know him.' That was a laugh! She knew every contour of him, every intonation of his voice, each expression . . .

'I don't know. I just thought maybe you and Mitch—well, you know, kind of liked each other,' Gemma finished lamely.

'Liked each other?' Ashleigh repeated. 'Disliked, you mean.'

'Oh, I know you're always arguing with him, but I can tell he rather likes you, Ash.'

'What makes you think that?' Ashleigh couldn't stop the question escaping.

'Well, he's always watching you. And he finds some excuse to be near you—things like that.' Gemma's cheeks were pink.

'Gem, please! You're imagining things. I can't stand a bar of him. And the feeling's mutual. He's exactly the type of man I abhor. He's so damn sure of himself, thinks every female that crosses his path is going to fall for him. In fact he expects it.' Ashleigh felt her anger rising. 'Well, I'm not going to join the queue! I wouldn't give him the satisfaction—not for a hundred Mitch Patricks!'

'I still say he fancies you,' Gem persisted.

'I don't fancy him.' Ashleigh wished wholeheartedly that she believed her forceful words.

Gemma didn't look convinced. 'Ashleigh, if you do like him.' She held up her hand when her sister went to deny it. 'No, wait, Ash. All I want to say is if you do like him don't let your pride stand in your way. Do you know what I'm trying to say?' Gemma's young face was red now.

Ashleigh sat down beside her sister and patted her arm. 'Yes, I know what you mean but—well, Mitch isn't like Joel. Joel loves and respects you. Mitch Patrick isn't interested in marriage and all the things we've been brought up to expect from a relationship, to respect. He's only interested in living for the moment, taking what he wants when it's available and discarding it when he tires of it or finds something else to amuse him.' She stood up again.

'Does he want to have an affair with you, Ash? Is that what you're trying to say?' Gemma's eyes went sympathetically to her sister.

'Something like that,' Ashleigh replied softly.

'Oh.' Gemma frowned. 'Are you . . . Will you, Ash? Have an affair with him, I mean?'

Ashleigh raised her hands and let them fall. 'No I don't think I could. Not without losing my self-esteem.' She sighed. 'I'd be lying if I said he didn't attract me physically—but that's not everything. I still can't like him, his attitude or his standards.' She felt tears in her eyes and blinked them back.

'Ash, I'm sorry. I didn't mean to upset you.'

'I'll have to get used to it,' Ashleigh shrugged. 'It'll pass.'

'I don't suppose there's any chance he'll—well, change his attitude?' asked Gemma.

'I can't see it. He wants me to change my mind, but he's not prepared to see anything my way, so . . .' She smiled wryly. 'Stalemate!'

They looked at each other, but before either of them could say any more there was a knock on their door.

'Ashleigh? Gemma?' Liv's voice took Ashleigh to the door to swing it open. 'Ready to go?' she beamed, looking beautiful in a loose black Empire line dress that complemented her long fair hair.

They set off along the beach to the hotel complex in the four-wheel-drive, although not before the seating arrangements had caused some amusement. The four-wheel-drive only seated six and there were seven of them. Ryan, who was driving, put Liv into the front beside him and Megan stated that she would sit quite comfortably on Mitch's knee. After all, she was the lightest, she told them. Ashleigh ended up in the middle of the back seat, her leg touching Mitch's, his shoulder against hers, and she closed her eyes, half of her wishing the evening was over and the other half of her savouring the bittersweetness of his touch, and calling herself all kinds of a fool to find any enjoyment in a situation where another girl was sitting balanced on Mitch's knee, other arms wrapped around his broad shoulders.

Their meal in the large restaurant was all Liv said it would be, and eventually they moved into the adjoining room where a band played a modern version of a familiar old ballad. Ryan led them to a table near some large open doors, and Ashleigh appreciated the cool breeze on her hot body. And she knew it wasn't the temperature or the humidity that was causing it.

All through their dinner she had been aware of dark blue eyes returning to watch her, starting the drumbeat of her pulse and the quickening of her breathing. By the time they had reached the dessert stage she could barely swallow each mouthful, and her anger rose.

How dared he? He was embarrassing her in front of everyone. Liv Denison had noticed how often Mitch's eyes strayed towards Ashleigh, and she knew Gemma was now aware of it.

Now she managed to sit beside Megan, with Mitch on the girl's other side, and, out of range of his watching eyes, she began to relax just a little. Overhead the ceiling fans rotated, circulating the air, and the sea breeze filtered in through the open doors. Ashleigh wished she could go outside and savour the moonlit night, but of course she couldn't take the chance of Mitch following her, putting her through more torment.

The band struck up a fast number and Megan pulled Mitch out of his seat and led him on to the dance floor. Joel and Gemma joined them and Liv moved so that she could talk to Ashleigh. They discussed the meal and the decor of the hotel, Ashleigh making sure she kept her eyes from the dance floor, not wanting to see Megan with Mitch, knowing the tentacles of jealousy would reach out to each part of her body, tightening painfully.

She danced a medium to slow number with Ryan and then Joel drew her on to the floor to partner him in a very modern disco beat. Joel threw himself into the dance with enthusiasm and Ashleigh began to relax, matching his exuberance with her own.

Flushed and laughing at the end of the first bracket, they decided to stay on the floor for the next one, and as the music began again Ashleigh glanced across at their table, her eyes meeting Mitch's, his eyes as black as coal, his expression grim and forbidding. The cold steeliness of his displeasure caused her step to falter momentarily, but she recovered herself, her gaze breaking from his as she turned her attention back to Joel. Who or what had upset him now?

When they rejoined the others Ashleigh fell into her seat, hot and breathless.

'You're not bad, Ashleigh,' Ryan congratulated her on her dancing efforts.

'For my advanced age, you mean?' Ashleigh teased.

'Ashleigh always was the best dancer in the family,' Gemma pointed out.

'Louise and Debbie could probably give me a run for my money now.' Ashleigh ran her fingers through her hair, damp from her exertions, lifting it from the back of her neck, letting the breeze cool her.

'Oh, Mitch, here's a romantic one. Can we do it?' asked Megan as the slow beat filled the room.

'Sorry, Megan.' He was standing up. 'I promised this one to Ashleigh,' he said, taking Ashleigh's arm and pulling her to her feet.

They were on the dance floor before Ashleigh had realised his intention.

'You don't care about anyone's feelings but your own, do you?' she snapped angrily as he pulled her into his arms so that she couldn't return to her seat and leave him in the middle of the floor, which was just what she wanted to do.

'You can talk,' he remarked shortly, putting her hand on his chest so that he had both hands free to settle disturbingly on her back, pulling her nearer.

'What do you mean?' She tried unsuccessfully to make some space between them. The movement of his hard body against hers was having its usual devastating effect on her equilibrium.

'I don't suppose you care that I felt like throttling Joel while you had such an exciting and enjoyable time with him on the dance floor?' he asked, his voice terse, his jaw tense, his hands tightening about her before he forced himself with obvious difficulty to relax a little.

'I was only dancing with him, nothing else.' Ashleigh watched a pulse beating beside his mouth. 'And you have no right to dictate to me, if it comes to that!'

'Ashleigh, I'm warning you . . .'

'Warning me? About what?' Ashleigh asked him quietly, angrily. 'My God, you've got a nerve! I'll say it again—you have no right to say a thing about who I choose to dance with.'

'Ashleigh!' he bit out before taking a steadying breath. 'We'd better just dance or I won't be responsible for my actions.'

Ashleigh opened her mouth to protest, but he cut her off.

'Just dance!' he said, moulding her closer.

For a few moments she remained tense in his arms, but the gentle sensuousness of the music, the insinuations of Mitch's body worked their magic, and soon she had relaxed involuntarily in his arms. Her arms slid around his waist so that her hands could move over the firmness of his back while his hands played down the length of her spine, teasing sensitive nerve endings, to settle on the roundness of her hips, and she gave herself up to the heady delight of the moment.

The rest of the dancers blurred into obscurity. The only other human being who existed for her was Mitch, his body strong and hard, pressed to the softness of hers, his breath warm and tantalising against her temple. Her eyes closed, her heart beating its song of arousal, allowing herself to drift where he guided her. They were the last two people on earth marooned in each other's arms.

The sudden coolness of the sea breeze **was** the first indication that they were outside in the moonlit semi-darkness. Ashleigh raised her head to look up at Mitch and when his head came down to claim her lips with his she met him halfway, unable to deny herself the sensation of his lips on hers. His teeth nibbled her bottom lip, slowly sliding around to tease her earlobe before returning to her trembling mouth again, her response inflaming him as his arms encircled her, crushing her to him. When their lips parted they were both breathless, and Ashleigh leant weakly against him, her knees showing signs of withdrawing their support.

'Ash! Ash!' he groaned. 'You're driving me crazy. I can't seem to get you out of my mind, awake or asleep.' His lips moved against the softness of her neck. 'Can't you feel what you do to me?' he asked thickly.

'Mitch, I . . .' Ashleigh knew full well what her nearness was doing to him, to herself, and she pushed her hands against his chest as she raised her eyes to his. She wanted so much to forget everything, but how long would his interest last? Slowly she shook her head and her breath caught on a sob. 'Oh, Mitch,' she whispered despairingly, and then took a deep breath. 'The music's stopped. We should go inside—we'll be missed.' Even as she said it her hands ran over the firmness of his chest, her fingers taking pleasure from the smoothness of his shirt stretched across hard muscles.

'Missed by whom? I couldn't care less, could you?' His lips continued their sensual exploration. 'We could go down to the beach and watch the sunrise. Shades of our little escapade,' he chuckled huskily, 'on the island.'

Escapade! That was exactly what it was, Ashleigh thought as her part in that night flooded back to taunt her. Her colour rose when she remembered how close she had come to, how close she always came to forgetting all her ideals, her moral standards when Mitch Patrick caressed her the way he was caressing her now.

'No!' Her own voice took her by surprise.

Mitch raised his head and tightened his arms about her when she would have pushed herself away. 'No what? No, we won't be missed or no to the beach?' His voice was deep and vital.

'I . . . I want to go inside.' Ashleigh's words fell over themselves in her agitation.

'For God's sake, Ashleigh! I've never met anyone who can blow as hot and cold as you can.' His voice mirrored his sudden anger and he pulled her back against him. 'Well, I'm sorry, but I can't seem to switch on and off as easily as you appear to be able to do.'

Ashleigh tried to turn her head away from his punishing lips, but he claimed them with a relentless demand. Her hands tried to push him away, but he held her suffocatingly close, his hard mouth forcing her lips against her teeth.

A sob rose in her throat and she moaned softly,

wanting him and hating him at the same time. When
he eventually raised his head he was breathing as
though he had been running and she felt his eyes
burning over her.

'God, I can't take much more of this,' he muttered
savagely, and thrust her from him. 'You'd better go
inside before I completely lose my head.'

'Where ... where are you going?' she asked as he
turned away from her, but he didn't bother to reply as
he strode across the pavement and disappeared into
the darkness.

For some moments Ashleigh stood and stared at the
blanket of night that had swallowed his tall figure and
she had to fight down the tears that threatened to
course down her cheeks. Her fingers went to her
bruised lips and blindly she turned back to the doorway, very nearly colliding with Megan as she strode
purposefully out through the open doors.

The two girls stood in the square of light that
escaped from the room and Megan's eyes narrowed
sharply, her eyes falling over Ashleigh's figure.

'I'm looking for Mitch,' she stated coldly.

'He ... he went towards the beach,' Ashleigh replied
haltingly, feeling her colour rise as she went to move
past the other girl.

'Has he been up to his old tricks?' Megan gave a soft
short laugh. 'He's a sensual devil, isn't he? But a word
of warning, Ashleigh. He's right out of your league, so
be careful you don't get singed!'

Ashleigh could only stare at the other girl.

'He often amuses himself with prim little ladies like
yourself. I think he looks upon it as something like
another mountain to climb, so don't take him too
seriously, will you?' Megan smiled.

'I can assure you Mitch Patrick would be the very last person I'd take seriously,' Ashleigh was stung to retort.

'I'm glad you're sensible, Ashleigh. Well, I'd better go and pick up the pieces again.' Megan went to walk off, a knowing smile on her face.

'You're right about one thing, though.' Ashleigh's words checked the other girl's steps and she raised an enquiring eyebrow. 'He does make an interesting and amusing . . . diversion, when one has nothing better to do.' With that parting remark Ashleigh continued into the dance hall.

By the time she reached their table she was feeling decidedly bitchy and half wished she hadn't allowed herself the luxury of that parting remark to Megan.

It was a good half hour before Mitch and Megan rejoined them, and after one quick glance at Mitch's face Ashleigh kept her attention on the dancers on the floor even though she wasn't really seeing them. Mitch had lit up a cigarette before taking his seat and resting his arm along the back of Megan's chair. As he exhaled a cloud of smoke his lids closed against the haze, Ashleigh's eyes met his. The corners of his mouth lifted cynically before he leant closer to Megan to catch something she said to him.

Her heart contracting painfully Ashleigh wished the evening was over, that the weekend had passed, and that she had reached the sanctuary of the rambling old Craig home in Brisbane. Even the plane journey south didn't hold as much trepidation for her. Anything to be away from the despair of the situation into which she'd fallen.

Later, lying in the unfamiliar bed, Ashleigh found the oblivion of sleep eluding her and she tossed restlessly. How could she have been so foolish as to allow herself to fall in love with Mitch Patrick?

Her eyes flew wide open in the darkness. In love with him? I don't even like him or what he is, she told herself. How could she be in love with him? Never in a million years could she like the type of man he was—arrogant, unprincipled, so self-orientated. In fact, he was everything she disliked intensely in a man. The exact opposite of Jonathan. Jonathan—hadn't she been so very sure she loved him? Then why did she have trouble bringing his face to mind? Why did Jonathan's face keep fading away, only to be replaced by the hard planes and angles of another face with bright dark blue eyes, square jaw and oh, so sensual lips that had aroused her so easily only short hours earlier?

It's purely physical, she cried, this yearning ache deep inside that drew her closer to him when she knew she should turn and run, clutch the last straw of self-preservation and put as much space between them as she could. Purely physical. Ashleigh put her hand to her face and her cheeks were wet with her tears.

God, she was a fool! A blind naïve fool! And she had no one to blame but herself. In the beginning she should have cut and run, gone straight back to Brisbane and Jonathan without giving Mitch Patrick the chance to disrupt her life.

Closing her eyes tightly, she tried to put it all from her mind, but of course it was no use. She couldn't go to sleep, and if she continued to lie here a moment longer she would go quietly insane.

Silently she climbed out of bed and pulled her short towelling robe over her nightie, tying the belt loosely around her waist. Gemma was sleeping peacefully and the only sounds were the occasional creak of expanding and contracting timber and the gentle rustle of the sea breeze in the trees and bushes outside.

Opening their bedroom door, Ashleigh padded on bare feet down the hallway and into the living-room. This room ran the width of the house with sliding glass doors at each end opening on to the courtyard and pool at the back and the patio and beach at the front. Ashleigh chose the latter and sliding the screens closed behind her she walked quietly down the steps, not stopping until she felt the still warm sand between her toes.

The bright almost full moon lit the white sand, highlighting the rippling of the water, and she longed to feel the salt water cooling her heated body. But she would never go swimming in the sea alone, especially at night. It would be foolhardy. She shivered at the thought. It was such a pity, though.

Sighing, she walked ruefully back to the house, and she had just closed the screens when she remembered the pool at the back of the house. Before giving herself time to stop and think she was back in the room she shared with Gemma and was slipping into her now dry bikini, grabbing her beach towel as she left.

The quarry tiles of the courtyard were cold to her bare feet after the shag pile carpet and the water of the pool made her shiver as she slid over the tiled edge and the coolness flowed about her hot body. Pushing away from the side, she struck out across the pool's width with slow leisurely strokes. After a couple of widths she rolled over on to her back, floating in the semi-darkness. The stars above twinkled in the dark sky and the sound of the ocean nearby began soothing her pressured mind.

What was she to do about her feelings for Mitch?

That was the question which kept revolving around inside her, slipping uninvited into her thoughts each time she let down her guard. Since she had admitted to herself that she was in love with him a little of the stress had left her. Now, she thought wryly, all she had to do was decide what to do about it. Feeling the way she did, she couldn't marry Jonathan, of that she was certain.

If she left on Monday and put all those miles between them would she be able to wipe him as easily from her mind? Somehow she doubted it.

Her stomach began to churn again. She would never have believed she could fall in love with a man like Mitch Patrick. Perhaps it was because he reminded her of Robbie and all that a first love meant. But although he had the same physical build and similar colouring to Robbie he was nothing like him in nature. Robbie had been a goodnatured, fun-loving boy, while Mitch was all hard, uncompromising man, overbearing, used to having his own way, expecting women to fall all over him. And, heaven help her, she was as weak as the rest.

Maybe if she did agree to have an affair with him she would be able to get him out of her system, break this hold he seemed to have on her. Break—that was the operative word. Once Mitch had tired of her he would make the break and loving him as she did that would be the unkindest cut of all. Better to sever the tie now before she learned to care too much.

A lump rose in her throat and she sighed dejectedly, propelling herself to the pool's edge. She supposed she should go back to bed and try to sleep out what was left of the night.

'And I always thought mermaids were completely

mythical beings!' a deep husky voice came out of the semi-darkness.

Fingers clutching the solid coolness of the brick-work, Ashleigh looked up at him as though he was a mirage, something she had conjured up because he had been continuously in her thoughts for what seemed like hours.

'What . . . what are you doing here?' Her voice was thick, unlike her own.

'Same as you, apparently. I couldn't sleep, so I came out for a swim.' He lowered his legs into the water and slid over the edge into the pool beside her, rippling the water around her.

Ashleigh stiffened, feeling her body flame at his nearness. Although the blue water separated them she tingled as though he had touched her. It was far too intimate.

'Mmm, that's better,' he said. 'Care to race me two or three lengths?'

'No. I've . . . I've already done a couple of lengths. I think . . . I think I'll get out. I'm tired enough to sleep now.' Her hands were on the pool's edge, her muscles flexing to draw herself upwards, when his hands settled on her bare waist, holding her back.

'Don't run away from me, Ash,' his warm breath teased her earlobe.

'I'm not running away,' she denied breathlessly, if not quite honestly. 'I . . . I would have been getting out anyway.'

His hands turned her around to face him. 'Ashleigh?' Her name was a conscious thought-destroying caress that set the blood pounding through her veins.

'Mitch, please,' she begged him softly, 'don't make it any harder for me than it is.'

'It doesn't have to be, you know that.' His hands pulled her to him, the feel of his hard body against hers dissolving her fragile defences with adept ease. 'Don't fight me, Ashleigh. Your body tells me we both want the same thing.' His hands played down the nakedness of her back, arching her impossibly closer to the slippery smoothness of his flat stomach and muscular thighs.

'Mitch, you don't understand,' Ashleigh began, only to have the words cut off as his lips came down to claim hers in a kiss that was passionately demanding and yet so dangerously persuasive.

He slowly raised his head. 'Isn't this all we need to understand?' he asked huskily, his thumbs caressing the wetness of her smooth midriff, evoking a shiver of aroused anticipation. 'Your body's telling me yes,' he added softly, his lips seeking the soft contours of her throat with practised persistence.

'Mitch, please! I can't think straight when you do that,' Ashleigh cried in despair.

'Then don't try to think straight. Let me carry you with me spiralling upwards,' he laughed huskily, his lips continuing their sensuous exploration down to the hollow between her breasts confined in her brief bikini top.

'I ... I'm still engaged to Jonathan,' she got out at last, and he raised his head to look down at her. 'I can't ... Mitch, I've decided to break my engagement when I go home, but—well, right now I'm still engaged to him. I ... I owe him ... I feel I owe him some ... Oh, Mitch, I have got principles, some code of morals, and I can't ...'

'You would have on the island,' he stated flatly, his hands not surrendering her as she tried to put some breathing space between them before his potent nearness completely eroded her willpower.

'We've been through all that,' she bit out. 'I wasn't myself. I . . . it was the delayed shock of the landing.'

Mitch's broad shoulders glistened in the moonlight and she shivered uncontrollably again.

'Ashleigh, for . . .'

'Let me go, Mitch. I'm cold—I want to go inside.' Her voice was almost steady.

'I could make you stay, Ashleigh,' he said evenly, 'make you want to stay. You know that.'

'Yes, you . . . you're probably right.' Her voice shook. More right than you know, she added to herself. 'But I'd have no self-respect left if I did stay,' she finished quietly.

His hands tightened for a moment and her pulses leapt, then he thrust her away, turning sharply away from her.

'Goodnight, Mitch,' Ashleigh said softly as she pulled herself shakily out of the pool, stopping to pick up her beach towel and wrap it sarong-wise around her.

'Ashleigh!' Her name spoken softly stopped her as she went to walk off. 'Your principles aren't going to keep you warm on a cold night,' he said evenly before he struck out for the opposite end of the pool.

CHAPTER NINE

ASHLEIGH had to drag herself from a web of sleep next morning feeling as though she had barely closed her eyes, and if anyone noticed she was slightly subdued, her face just a little pinched, no comment was made. A couple of times she felt Gemma's eyes move worriedly over her, but her sister asked no questions, instinctively realising Ashleigh had no desire to discuss her troubles.

Gemma assured them that her bruised knee was much better, so right after lunch Ashleigh, Gemma and Joel set off along the beach, with Ashleigh trying valiantly to convince herself she was happy Mitch had decided not to join their languid beachcombing; that it hadn't disturbed her to see him stretched out by the pool beside Megan, the sun glistening on the contours of his bronzed body, highlighting the perfect symmetry of his hard muscles, the latent strength that emanated from him, that flowed about him like a magnetic aura.

Eventually they were back aboard *Midnight Blue* cutting across the salty blueness towards Shute Harbour. Sitting with the wind in her hair, seeming to enjoy the sensation of sun and speed, it was easy for Ashleigh to isolate herself from the conversation. She wanted to think but shied from thought, making a valiant attempt to keep her mind a blank.

She seemed to be able to manage it most of the time until she turned her head slightly and her eyes skittered over Mitch's figure as he moved about adjusting the rigging or simply stood gazing out over the blue sky and sea, his own thoughts an enigma.

Then her mind revved in neutral, spun ineffectually without finding a forward or reverse. And the questions piled in one upon the other, bombarding her vulnerable heart with relentless consistency until she looked away, averted her eyes to some other point, some object that had no painful associations.

She had been giving her attention to a shining chrome bollard, methodically watching the changing reflections in its brightly gleaming surface, when the hair on the back of her neck began to prickle urgently and she knew he was quite near. Forcing herself to keep her eyes from being drawn to him was an impossibility, and swallowing a rush of self-derision at her weakness she turned her head and their eyes met. Mitch's glowed intensely, the surrounding blueness reflected in his irises, as bright as blue sapphires.

Ashleigh felt herself begin to tremble all over as her senses tuned in to his silent song, his eyes caressing her with implacable thoroughness. She almost moaned his name, her white teeth biting into her lower lip to hold back her response. To tear her eyes away from him was a physical pain that left in its wake a throbbing ache within her. If she stayed anywhere near him, how long would it be before she surrendered, gave up the fight she was having with all the ideals she thought she held dear, before she allowed him to have his way?

And if she admitted the truth she was also fighting herself. Her own body betrayed her each time he touched her, at the sound of his deep voice. Her attraction to him was wearing her away, eroding her like the action of water on a stone. She was losing ground in his sensual attack upon her senses, so the sooner she broke away from his almost gravitational pull, simply left the area, the better.

'Isn't the weather divine up here, Ash?' Gemma broke into Ashleigh's thoughts.

'Oh—sorry, Gem, I was thinking about something else.' Her eyes went back to Mitch before she could stop herself and his eyes were watching her again.

'Gem was commenting on the great weather,' said Mitch, lounging back against part of the cabin structure. 'Nice hot days, even though the nights can be cold.' A mocking smile played around the corners of his mouth as his eyes slid over her body, catapulting the evening before so graphically into her mind.

'Cold nights are for breaking out my electric blanket.' Ashleigh met his eyes levelly.

'And our flannelette nighties,' laughed Gemma, blushing slightly as Mitch's gaze swung to her and one fair eyebrow rose.

'The mind boggles,' he said amusedly. 'Not the neck-to-floor variety surely?' he asked.

'I'm afraid so,' Ashleigh said while Gemma was embarrassedly trying to decide how to answer him. 'Neck to wrist to floor. Very warm on cold nights.'

'Pity you won't be here in winter, Ashleigh. I'm sure we could show you alternative ways of keeping warm on a cool night.' The tone of his voice left no doubt to the insinuations of his words.

'I'm sure you could.' Ashleigh kept her own voice even. 'What a pity I'm returning home tomorrow.' Her eyes met his then, telling him just how glad she was to be going, and his body tensed imperceptibly, his lips thinning.

Gemma blushed profusely, her eyes going to the deck. 'It would have been great if you could have spent your whole school vacation up here, Ash,' she got out jerkily, attempting to cover her embarrassment.

'Ashleigh's fiancé,' Mitch paused slightly over the word, 'may have had something to say about that,' he stated as he stood up abruptly and rejoined Ryan at the wheel.

'Oh dear!' Gemma's young face filled with anxiety. 'He's . . . he's upset again.'

'Tough!' Ashleigh ejaculated between clenched teeth. 'It's only his wounded ego talking. One of his toys won't play the game by his rules, that's all.'

A frown puckered Gemma's brow as she watched her sister walk to the opposite end of the yacht to where Mitch was and stretch out on the deck to sunbake.

'Ashleigh? You awake?' Joel's voice brought her back from the cobwebby euphoria of peaceful dozing.

'Mmm!' She sat up slowly, rubbing her eyes, still gritty from her sleepless night.

'We've just picked up a message on the radio and it seems like you've got a visitor,' Joel said quietly as Gemma joined them.

'A visitor? Where?' Ashleigh came fully awake. 'What do you mean, Joel?' She looked from his face to Gemma.

'Back at the Harbour. There's someone waiting for you.'

'Waiting for . . .? Who?' Ashleigh asked incredulously, wondering if she was dreaming.

'Jonathan Randall.' Joel was watching her carefully, obviously trying to gauge her reaction.

'Jonathan? Here? But . . . Are you sure, Joel?' Ashleigh couldn't take it in.

'Mitch and I heard it with our own ears,' he replied.

At the sound of Mitch's name Ashleigh flushed a

little. 'But how did he . . .?'

'Apparently he arrived here last night by car, so he'll be waiting at the wharf when we get back.'

'Last night?' Ashleigh seemed to be repeating everything parrot fashion. 'Oh! He . . . he wouldn't have expected me to be . . . to be away.'

'You weren't to know Jonathan would be coming up here, Ash,' Gemma patted her shoulder.

'No. No, I wasn't, she said almost reflectively, and then pulled herself together, putting a smile on her face. 'Well, that's a surprise. How long before we're back at Shute Harbour?'

'Half hour or so,' smiled Joel. 'You sound pleased to hear he's waiting for you.'

Heavens, could Joel be so wrong? Ashleigh looked up into Mitch's chiselled features as he walked up behind Joel. 'I am,' she said with as much conviction as she could muster. It wasn't strictly an untruth. At least they could talk about their relationship and she could try to explain to Jonathan that she couldn't marry him. But in the sense Joel meant her confirmation was an abject lie.

'Can you give me a hand with the mainsail, Joel?' Mitch drew Joel's attention.

'Sure.' Joel moved forward and Gemma stood up to follow him.

'So!' Mitch spoke quietly, between his teeth. 'Enter the knight in shining armour astride his snow-white charger,' he said, his deep voice thick with sarcasm. 'Poor Sir Jonathan! And the damsel isn't even in distress.'

Before Ashleigh could retaliate he had walked after Joel and Gemma, leaving Ashleigh sitting on the deck angered and uncertain.

They were so close to the wharf now that she could pick out Jonathan's still figure standing beside his car, his darkish hair lifting uncharacteristically in the breeze. She couldn't as yet make out his expression, but he held himself stiffly erect and she felt a wave of guilt wash over her.

Feeling a pulse beating in the hollow of her throat, she clutched at the rail and tried to swallow her nervousness. What was she going to say to him? How was she going to tell him she no longer wanted to get married?

Perhaps she should amend that statement, she told herself self-derisively. She no longer wanted to marry him—that was the real point. If she admitted the truth, she wanted to marry Mitch Patrick, but he didn't want to marry her. And that was something she'd have to learn to live with.

Her eyes swung sideways to meet Mitch's, unaware of the sadness in her expression, and he walked across to stand beside her, his gaze on the wharf that was growing closer with each minute.

Ashleigh steeled herself, waiting for him to make a cynical remark, but he simply stood there silently until she thought her nerve ends would explode her complete emotional turmoil.

'We're almost there,' she said when his silence became an agony she could no longer bear.

He turned his head, his eyes settling on her face, his expression as enigmatic as usual. 'You don't appear to be looking forward to the coming reconciliation,' he remarked flatly.

Ashleigh flinched, hating his apparent indifference, not able to find an equally wounding retaliation.

'Poor devil! I can almost pity him,' his voice was

low and bitter. 'All this way for nothing. And you're going to hit him with a broken engagement as well. Maybe you should reconsider that decision before you burn all your bridges.'

'Maybe I already have reconsidered my decision,' Ashleigh replied, her voice clipped, trying to disguise the pain that clutched at her heart.

His eyes raked her, and her anger rose. She wanted to hurt him as he was hurting her.

'Have you?' he asked softly, his tone disbelieving, his eyes returning to the direction of the wharf and Jonathan.

'Yes, I have,' she threw back at him. 'And perhaps I've decided that eight years of knowing someone, knowing you have a lot in common, knowing that he wants to protect you, that he respects you, means more than a couple of days of physical attraction.' She heard Mitch's breath rasp in his throat and watched him slowly turn back to her. 'That's all it is—a biological affinity we seem to have for each other on the lowest level.'

'I see.' His voice was cold and quiet. 'Just a sin of the flesh.'

'You *are* physical, Mitch. That's why you do so well attracting members of the opposite sex. It's grown to be almost a trade mark with you. You switch it on and every woman succumbs.' Ashleigh laughed mirthlessly. 'Even me. But don't come to depend on that physical attraction too much in case you lose the knack. That's when everyone will want to see what's underneath.' Her eyes raked him in turn. 'And I've got a feeling that beneath all that pure sex there's nothing, an empty shell. Is that the reason you shun lasting relationships, Mitch? Because you don't want anyone to discover your little secret? Because . . .'

'Ashleigh, that's enough,' he broke in.

'Did I get too close to the truth that time?' Ashleigh goaded, unable to stop herself now that she had begun, a small part of her recognising from some position way off from herself that she was bordering on hysteria.

'I'm beginning to think you wouldn't know the truth if it stared you in the face!' His words were forced out between his teeth.

She could tell he was only just holding his own anger in check and she laughed again. 'My barbs have pierced your thick hide, haven't they? And you don't like it!'

'You're pushing me too far, Ashleigh, and what's more you know you're doing it.' His head rose and his eyes narrowed. 'I wonder why?'

Her taunting gaze faltered slightly and he took immediate advantage of it.

'Do you want me to do your dirty work, is that it?' His voice had changed, was more controlled, as though he now had himself under a tighter rein.

'What . . . What do you mean?'

'I mean good old Jonathan.' He moved his fair head slightly in the direction of the wharf. 'Haven't you got the guts to tell him yourself? You want to goad me into some form of physical display; physical being the colour you so vehemently paint me; that will leave him in no doubt about where the land lies? Well, have I hit the nail on the head?'

'Why, you . . .'

'Don't chicken out now, Ashleigh, not when you've come so far.' His smile lifted the corners of his mouth but didn't go even close to his eyes. 'Okay, here I am! Right where you want me.' His tone was as cold as steel. 'But it's going to have to come from you. If you want to use me to break it to him you'll have to make the first move. You'll have to do it yourself and you'll have to do it now. We're closing fast, and if you leave it too late it will look contrived, and I'm sure you don't want that, do you? Well, Ashleigh? All you need to do is put your arms around me, nothing as showy as a passionate kiss.'

Her eyes met his then and she felt her lips tremble and had to bite her bottom lip to hold back the cry of pain his cruelty had caused. They stood staring at each other, while the rest of the world about them slithered by like the salt water along the side of the yacht's sleek hull. Tears flooded Ashleigh's eyes and his face blurred before her. Blinking quickly, she tried to prevent them from spilling over, but one escaped to trickle coldly down her flushed cheek, a bright golden-tinged jewel in the setting sunlight.

'Ashleigh?' His voice sounded constricted, as though his throat had closed, and she raised a hand to dash the dampness from her eyes.

His hand covered hers as it clutched back at the rail and his grip tightened, momentarily punishing. 'Ash?' He stopped, and releasing her hand he turned and flung away from her.

As the yacht nudged the wharf Ashleigh saw Jonathan straighten from the car and begin walking across the car park. She stood transfixed, fighting for control, forcing back the tears that continued to sting her eyes. She had to pull herself together.

'Are you ready, Ash?' Gemma asked quietly, coming to stand beside her sister.

'I'll have to collect my things,' Ashleigh began.

'That's okay. Joel's got our bags and I've got our dresses.'

Jonathan met them as they disembarked and resting his hands momentarily on Ashleigh's shoulders he kissed her on the cheek. Her voice stuck fast in her throat, but with everyone milling around her silence passed unnoticed until she had to rouse herself to make all the introductions.

'I suppose you'll want to go back to the flat with Jonathan, Ashleigh,' Joel said brightly.

Glancing sideways at Jonathan, she nodded, wondering if she was imagining the sharp look he was giving her. She was trying desperately to stop herself from making comparisons between Jonathan and Mitch, but it was inevitable. She had made her comparisons subconsciously before she could prevent herself doing it.

In dark slacks and crisp white shirt, neat and trim as always, Jonathan should have come out the better, but somehow Ashleigh rather suspected that he had been left behind, that the choice had been made before her conscious mind had recognised the decision.

As he stood silently, his face expressionless, his hair windblown, bleached almost white from the sun, clad in faded denim shorts and an old T-shirt that had seen better days, it was as though Mitch reached out and touched her, put a seal upon her heart, excluding anyone else. He simply stood alone, brooking no comparison.

'If we all push off now,' Joel was saying, glancing at his wristwatch, 'we should be able to shower and change and make it down to the pub for dinner. How about it?'

'Better count us out,' said Ryan. 'Liv's had a big enough weekend as it is. I think we'll opt for a quiet evening at home.'

'Okay. What about you, Mitch?' Joel turned to his cousin, his eyes just faintly wary.

'We'd love to, wouldn't we, darling?' Megan purred, hanging on to Mitch's free arm.

Mitch's eyes went over Ashleigh and Jonathan, not giving a suspicion of his feelings, before he turned back to Megan. 'If you like,' he said noncommittally.

'Actually, I did hope to get some free time with Ashleigh,' Jonathan began.

'I'd like to go, Jon,' Ashleigh put in hurriedly, cursing herself for her cowardice, clutching at anything that could delay the moment when she would have to tell him about her change of heart. About Mitch Patrick. She shot a sideways glance at Mitch and she read in his eyes a momentary eloquence, leaving her in no doubt that he was seeing right through her, into the deep turbulence of her troubled thoughts.

'All right, my dear,' Jonathan capitulated, a slight frown on his brow. 'I suppose we do have to eat somewhere.'

'Good. Well, let's get going, then.' Joel was lightly cheerful. 'See you all at the hotel in an hour or so.'

Ashleigh thanked Ryan and Liv for the weekend and then found herself seated beside Jonathan in his car, heading back towards Airlie Beach. Her mouth felt dry and her hands clutched rigidly together in her lap.

'I'm . . . I'm sorry I wasn't here when you arrived,' she began. 'If I'd known you were driving all this way I wouldn't have gone with Gemma,' she said quickly, feeling her pulse hammering in her throat.

'Yes. It was pretty much bad timing all round.' Jonathan sounded just slightly piqued.

'You didn't so much as hint that you might be coming up here when I spoke to you on the phone the other night,' said Ashleigh, by way of some excuse.

'I hadn't even thought about it then,' Jonathan said flatly.

'What . . . what made you come? I . . . I thought you were fairly busy at present.' Ashleigh tried to force herself to relax.

'I was. I still am,' he replied. 'I've been working towards having everything tied up before our wedding,' he said calmly.

A shock wave of guilt rose to consume her and she sat miserably in her seat, not knowing what to say or do.

'You do recall the date of our proposed marriage, don't you, Ashleigh?' Jonathan's voice was tinged with heavy sarcasm and it brought her eyes around to him in shock. 'Well, Ashleigh?' His eyes stayed on the road as he drove slowly along.

'Of course.' She swallowed. 'Of course I remember. Why . . . why do you ask that?'

'I thought you would be able to tell me,' he said. 'We've known each other a long time and I think I can tell when something's amiss with you. On the telephone the other night I felt some vibes, but I couldn't put my finger on just what the trouble was. So. Here I am. And I'd like us to discuss whatever it is before things get any worse.'

'Oh, Jon, I'm sorry. I . . .' Ashleigh turned blindly to gaze out of the passenger side window. 'I don't know what's wrong with me. I seem to have had a complete upheaval in the whole direction of my life.'

'You want to call the wedding off?' It was just short of a statement although Jonathan didn't outwardly seem to be agitated as he said the words. In fact he was being very matter-of-fact about it, the majority of his attention appearing to be taken up with his driving.

'I . . . I think it would be best.' Ashleigh couldn't look at him. 'I don't think it would be fair on you if we went ahead with it, with me feeling the way I do.'

'And how do you feel, Ashleigh? I think I'm entitled to some explanation, don't you?' A note of censure had entered his tone.

'I . . . Oh, I don't know, Jon, that's the point. I just don't feel as sure as I used to that I want to be married. I . . .' Ashleigh's voice faded away.

'Is there anyone else?' he asked quietly, after a few moments' silence.

'Not the way you mean,' she replied carefully.

'Come now, Ashleigh, either there is or there isn't. There's no half measures about that,' he said sharply as they pulled up in front of Gemma's flat.

'There's no one else that I'm going to marry. I just . . . I just don't think I . . . love you enough to marry you.' She put her hand on the door handle.

'Love!' he ejaculated angrily. 'We're hardly children, Ashleigh. We're past all that heated passion. I thought we would be building our life on a firmer foundation than that.'

'I thought so too, believe me,' Ashleigh said honestly, 'but now I know it wouldn't have worked, Jon. We'd both end up feeling cheated and dissatisfied.'

'Ashleigh, this is ridiculous! You're talking nonsense. When you came up here there was none of this in the offing, and I can't understand what's brought it all on now,' he said shortly.

'Maybe these few days apart gave me time to look at us without any distractions.' Ashleigh cringed inwardly as the word came out. Distractions. Mitch Patrick had been one big distraction from the moment she'd met him. 'Jonathan, I . . .'

'Look, I think we should leave it until later. The car is no place to discuss this.' Jonathan drummed his fingers irritably on the steering wheel. 'You'd better go in and change. I'll pick you up in three-quarters of an hour or so. I've just about worn a path between here and the hotel looking for you.'

'How did you know we'd gone sailing?' Ashleigh asked him glad of a short reprieve.

'I eventually decided to call the Denisons, hoping I'd reach Gemma's fiancé. Fortunately Mr Dension was at home and he filled me in.'

Ashleigh sighed. 'Jon, I'm sorry . . .'

'We'll discuss it after dinner,' he said firmly. 'Actually, you may as well come back to the hotel with Denison. I suppose he'll be collecting Gemma, so I'll see you there later.' And Ashleigh was left to climb out of the car and go inside.

Searching through the few dresses she'd brought along with her, she felt overcome with despair. She hadn't meant to hurt Jonathan in any way, but no matter which course she chose she *was* going to hurt him badly. He had trusted her and yet in one short week she had betrayed that trust. Perhaps she should go through with their wedding. Her hand stilled on the folds of her dress. Of course she couldn't go through with it. Better to make the break and save more hurt as time went on. Jonathan didn't deserve anything less than her truthfulness about Mitch Patrick.

'Ashleigh?' Gemma's voice broke in on her. 'Can't you decide what to wear?'

'Not exactly. I'm pretty limited as I only brought

three dresses with me and I don't feel much like wearing the one I wore last night.' Ashleigh schooled her features before she turned to her sister. 'But the other two aren't exactly suitable, so I guess I'll have to wear it.'

'I've got just the thing. I bought it ages ago and I've never worn it.' Gemma dived into her wardrobe and searched about, her voice coming muffled from the folds of her clothes. 'When I got it home and tried it on again I didn't think it suited me, so I haven't even taken up the hem.' She straightened and pulled out a pale green sheath. 'There. I bet it'll fit you perfectly, Ashleigh, you're taller than I am. Try it on.'

She had the silky dress over Ashleigh's head before her sister could demur. Gemma was right, it did fit perfectly. The dress could have been made for Ashleigh. The soft material hugged her full figure, accentuating her curves, and the slit up one side of the long straightish skirt displayed a length of tanned leg.

'Wow! I wish it looked that good on me,' grinned Gemma admiringly.

'Oh, Gem, I can't wear your new dress,' Ashleigh began, but Gemma waved that aside.

'You can have it. It's not me, anyway. Besides, I'd say you could use all the moral support you can get tonight, couldn't you?'

Her sister nodded and slowly began to brush her hair. 'I've told Jonathan,' she said softly. 'In the car on the way to the flat.'

'How did he take it?'

'Not well,' Ashleigh shrugged. 'But it had to be done. I just wish he hadn't driven all the way up here. I feel such a heel. It ... it wasn't, it won't be easy,' she added softly.

'You didn't ask him to come up here, Ash,' Gemma repeated.

'I know. But . . .' Ashleigh sighed. 'I'm not looking forward to this evening.'

'Ash, what about Mitch?' Gemma asked.

'What about him?' Ashleigh turned away so that her sister wouldn't see the pain she knew had to be in her eyes.

'Are you . . . I mean, have you told Jonathan about him?'

'No. What's there to tell?' Ashleigh ran her hand gently down the folds of her dress as she turned back to Gemma with more nonchalance than she was feeling. 'That I've made a complete and utter fool of myself over a modern-day Casanova who likes to love them when the mood takes him and leave them when he's bored with them? No, I don't think I'll tell Jonathan that. It wouldn't make things any easier. On him,' she laughed humourlessly, 'or my pride. What's left of it, that is.'

'Oh, Ash, I'm sorry.' Gemma's face mirrored her compassion. 'I feel kind of responsible somehow. If Mother hadn't been worried about me than she wouldn't have pressured you into leaving Brisbane and Jonathan and you would never have met Mitch.'

'Of course it's not your fault, Gem,' Ashleigh hastened to reassure her sister. 'If my relationship with Jon couldn't stand up to a few days' separation then it was better that we find out before we were married than afterwards, don't you think?'

'I guess so,' Gemma agreed reluctantly. 'And you still would have met Mitch eventually,' she added, 'at Joel's and my wedding. He's Joel's cousin, after all, and Joel would want him to be invited.'

A knock on the door of the flat interrupted them and Gemma turned to answer it. 'That'll be Joel.' She paused before she left the room. 'Keep your chin up, Ash. No matter what, you have to be true to yourself. It would be the biggest mistake to marry Jonathan if you're not absolutely sure you want to, even if Mitch wasn't involved.'

Ashleigh slowly slipped on her high sandals and left the bedroom. But Mitch was involved. And only Ashleigh knew how much.

'Are you coming with us, Ashleigh?' asked Joel, his eyes full of sympathy. Obviously Gemma had put him in the picture in the few moments they had had alone together before Ashleigh joined them but he made no comment and made no mention of Jonathan or Mitch.

'If you don't mind, Joel.' Ashleigh was beginning to feel a little like a piece of driftwood that nobody wanted, and she knew that was unfair on Joel, who showed no sign of not wanting her along to make a threesome.

'Of course I don't,' Joel smiled at her. 'Who'd knock the chance to escort two of the prettiest girls in town in to dinner? Not me, that's for sure!'

Joel's easy manner as they drove into Airlie Beach soothed Ashleigh's frayed nerves, and it was only as they went to climb the steps of the hotel that her tummy began to churn about with nervous distress and her steps faltered. However, Joel came to her rescue again, gently teasing as they stepped into the dining room.

Steeling herself unconsciously, Ashleigh felt her nerves stretch, but it was all unnecessary as they were the first to arrive. Joel led them across to the table he had reserved and the waiter had only just delivered their drinks when Jonathan joined them. His face was slightly stiff and uncommunicative, his eyes refusing to meet Ashleigh's, and her spirits sank guiltily.

The two men began to indifferently discuss the area and its seemingly skyrocketing progress in recent years, and by the time Mitch and Megan put in an appearance Ashleigh's nerves were screaming. Her mouth felt dry and she had trouble swallowing and her face felt pale and pinched.

The consultation of the menus covered a lot of the initial uneasiness which descended on the group as Mitch and Megan seated themselves beside Joel, and as soon as the waiter departed the tension returned. Ashleigh's eyes skipped over the others, she wondered if they were as aware of the strained atmosphere as she was or if it was only her own guilty conscience that was conjuring it up inside her imagination.

Apart from one brief glance when he arrived she had managed not to have to look at Mitch, but that one brief moment had been enough to corrode her self-control. Even now her hands were clasped tightly together beneath the table to still their trembling, and only by tensing her jaw could she prevent her teeth from chattering.

Her memory re-ran that one quick glance over and over, painting an indelible picture behind her eyes, adding each minute detail with graphic strokes—the slight curl at the ends of his fair hair still damp from his shower, the fine fair arch of his brows above deep blue eyes, bright liquid indigo, the proud straightness of his nose, lips slightly thinned although hinting at the sensual fullness she knew burned close to the surface—the strong square jaw, the firm bulge of strong muscular shoulders and arms, the flat midriff and narrow waist and the hardness of thighs that she could even now feel imprinted against her. Now her whole body was threatening to tremble and she bit her lip in an effort to regain her composure.

'Are you all right, Ash?' asked Gemma under cover of the conversation, but before Ashleigh could answer Jonathan had turned a frowning face on her.

'Aren't you well, Ashleigh?' he asked sternly.

'I'm . . . I'm fine.' Her eyes flicked to Mitch, but he was gazing at the smouldering end of his cigarette, apparently uninterested in the question or her answer.

'I hope you aren't suffering any ill-effects after your crash landing?' Jonathan persisted, watching her so closely she began to feel like a fly on the end of a pin.

'No, none at all,' she said with more conviction than she felt. No physical after-effects, jeered a voice inside her. 'And it wasn't exactly a crash landing.'

'Definitely not a crash landing,' agreed Joel, grinning across at Mitch. 'Just Mitch doing a fair imitation of the Red Baron, a role he seems to enjoy playing.'

Jonathan's attention focused sharply on Mitch for the first time. 'So you were the pilot of the plane. I must congratulate you on what sounded like a competent piece of flying. Ashleigh tells me you did a fine job landing on the beach.'

'Thanks.' Mitch exhaled a small haze of smoke. 'The situation wasn't as bad as it appeared to be,' he said flatly.

'What's all this about?' Megan's eyes went from Ashleigh to Mitch.

'Mitch was flying Ashleigh out over the islands last week and they got caught in a rain squall and had to put down on a beach. That's how he came by the interesting scratch on his cheek.' Joel grinned teasingly at his cousin. 'Mitch'll do anything for the chance to show off in front of a fair damsel, won't you, mate? Never known him let a chance pass him by!'

'Mitch! You didn't tell me,' pouted Megan. 'You could have been killed!' Her hand ran insinuatively over his arm.

'No such luck!' Mitch remarked drily, his eyes momentarily moving across to Ashleigh.

'Don't say that—it's too horrible to think about!' Megan pulled a face at him. 'How long did you have to sit out the storm?'

There was an infinitesimal pause before Mitch answered casually, 'About seventeen hours. It was dark before the rain stopped and then we had a couple of hours repair on the plane next morning before we could lift off.'

'You mean you spent the whole night on the island together?' Megan's implications were not veiled and Ashleigh felt her heart plummet. Red stained her cheeks and she looked up to see Jonathan's eyes narrowed on her face before he turned back to Mitch.

'Yes. Luckily Joel and I had used the island a few months before and the rough shelter we made was still habitable and mostly waterproof, so we were reasonably comfortable,' Mitch finished evenly, stubbing out his cigarette in the ashtray.

'Well, quite an adventure for you, Ashleigh,' Megan remarked, pausing over the word 'adventure', giving it all manner of meaning.

'As I'm not a very enthusiastic flier I'd call it more of a nightmare than an adventure,' said Ashleigh, using all her will-power to keep a light casualness in her voice. That Megan was thinking the worst about that night was so obvious that Ashleigh felt cheap and humiliated. Yes, nightmare was most definitely the right word, and how she wished she could completely eradicate that self-denigrating part of the nightmare from her so vivid and fertile memory.

'It was fortunate you didn't catch pneumonia,' put in Gemma. 'You very well could have, getting soaked to the skin.'

Fully expecting Mitch to remark blandly that they had shed their wet clothes, Ashleigh looked apprehensively at his face, and if the sardonic lifting of one fair eyebrow was any indication he knew what she expected of him.

'We managed to keep warm,' he said ambiguously, and Ashleigh felt herself cringe inwardly.

'Oh, I can imagine.' Megan's voice was cold and her eyes burned as they met Ashleigh's.

At the other girl's tone Gemma sat up straighter in her chair, bright pink circles appearing in her cheeks. 'Luckily Mitch had a survival kit in the plane,' she said directly at Megan. 'The hot soup and blankets were a godsend.'

There was a brief pause before Jonathan turned away from Ashleigh. 'I believe you landed on the island as well, Joel?'

Joel nodded. 'I suspected Mitch would have made for the island, so we tried there first and bingo! Right first time.' His infectious grin brought a little relief from the strain of a few moments earlier.

'I was terrified we wouldn't find them there.' Gemma closed her eyes. 'I was never more pleased to see anyone in my life than I was to see Mitch on that beach. When I think of what could have happened . . .' She shuddered.

'Well, it didn't happen,' Ashleigh found her voice,

'so stop worrying, Gem. I'll have lots to tell my class next year and I hope I'll be able to show them the photos I took of the reefs and islands.'

After that the conversation remained on neutral topics and Ashleigh allowed her tensed muscles to relax a little, although much of the talk went over her head as she sat in a weary limbo, willing the evening to end.

Eventually Mitch gave a barely concealed yawn, tiredly flexing his shoulders. 'Well, I think we'll push off. It's been a long weekend. Ready, Megan?'

'Oh, Mitch, don't be a party pooper! The night's still young.' She pouted, her small hands again encircling Mitch's muscular arm. 'Can't we find somewhere else where there's a bit more action?'

'This isn't King's Cross,' Mitch replied drily, getting to his feet so that the girl was forced to do likewise. 'I have to work tomorrow, so I'd appreciate a relatively early night.'

'Oh, all right,' said Megan with undisguised ill-grace. 'How do you stand all this fast living?' she asked sarcastically, her lips tight.

'I sometimes wonder,' he replied almost inaudibly, his eyes going to Ashleigh, flicking her so easily on the raw. 'Goodnight, all.' And he had ushered Megan out of the dining room before anyone could do more than repeat his farewell.

'I guess we should be making a move too, love,' said Joel, his arm going around Gemma's shoulders. 'It's back to work for you tomorrow as well.'

'Ugh! That's right. I'd almost succeeded in conveniently forgetting it,' grinned Gemma. 'How long do you have off work, Jonathan?' she asked. 'I mean, when do you plan on driving back down to Brisbane?'

'I have to be back for an important appointment on

Tuesday,' he said, a frown on his face.

'Oh.' Gemma's smile faltered a little. 'What about you, Ash? Coming home with Joel and me, or will you drive back to the flat with Jonathan?'

'I'll drive Ashleigh home,' Jonathan replied. 'Ashleigh and I have a few things we want to discuss,' he added, not even glancing in Ashleigh's direction.

'All right. Well,' Gemma paused indecisively, 'I . . . we'll see you later, Ash. I gave you the spare key to the flat, didn't I?'

Ashleigh nodded, and as Gemma and Joel left them her spirits sank. How she wished she could get up and run after them, not face the coming inquisition, but of course she couldn't evade it. She owed Jonathan more than that.

CHAPTER TEN

A HEAVY silence had fallen on them with the departure of the other two. The sounds of the remaining diners, the talk, the laughter, the clink of cutlery, made no impression on Ashleigh's hearing processes. She was only aware of the thick tension-laden stillness that had wrapped itself about herself and Jonathan.

'It appears you've packed a lot of happenings into just a few short days.' The sound of Jonathan's voice made Ashleigh jump and she swallowed convulsively.

'Jon, I . . .'

'You know, I've had a totally different impression of you these past years, and I can't decide which is the real you, Ashleigh, the woman I thought I knew well enough to ask her to share the rest of my life with me or the woman who seems to be pulling out all stops in an effort to have her last fling.'

'That's not fair, Jon. What have I done that's so bad? Good grief, I didn't manufacture that rain storm!' Ashleigh's anger rose, illogically fanned by the flash of memory that reminded her that it had crossed her mind at the time to blame the rain squall on Mitch Patrick.

'There's no need to raise your voice, Ashleigh.' Jonathan glanced about him at the nearby diners. 'I suggest we retire to the privacy of my room before you create even more of a scene.'

'Before I create . . .' Ashleigh repeated incredulously, her voice an angry whisper. 'Jon, I don't think this is the time to discuss anything at all, not while you're in this antagonistic biased state of mind. We wouldn't achieve a thing.' She stood up and began to walk past their table and out of the room, but Jonathan was beside her before she had taken a half dozen steps, his hand firmly grasping her arm.

'I haven't driven all this way to be put off so easily, Ashleigh,' he breathed furiously beside her, matching his step to hers. 'We're going to talk, whether you want to or not!' He continued to hold her arm as he led her down a corridor to his room, only releasing her when he stopped to fumble in his pocket for his key.

They were both coldly silent as he unlocked the door and flicked on the light, standing back for her to precede him inside. Ignoring the single chair in the hotel room, Ashleigh crossed to stand at the open screened window, staring out at the mass of greenery that grew in tangled disorder in the small patch of illuminated garden.

'There's no point in arguing, Jon. I'm sorry you came all this way, but I didn't ask you to come,' she said firmly.

'No, you didn't ask me to come up here. And I can see why. Sorry I turned up to spoil everything.' His lips curled derisively.

'Jon, how many times do I have to say it?' Ashleigh turned back to him. 'There's nothing to spoil.'

'Humph!' he ejaculated. 'Not from where I see it. What did you plan on doing, Ashleigh, if I hadn't turned up? Write me a "Dear John" letter or some other cowardly little evasion?'

Ashleigh sighed, forcing herself to keep calm. 'I was going to tell you when I came back to Brisbane on Monday. Tomorrow.'

'I'll bet you were. Tomorrow there would have been

more excuses about planes or buses so you could stay and flit about with some joy-riding daredevil pilot.'

'I was not flitting about! That's a ridiculous exaggeration, and you'd know it was too if you'd only stop ranting and raving and think about it rationally.' Ashleigh raised her hands and let them fall. 'If Mitch Patrick hadn't been such a good pilot then we might have been at the bottom of the ocean by now. You're simply clutching at any straw you can find because you're angry with me.'

'Angry! What did you expect from me, Ashleigh? That I'd bow and say "Oh well! That's life!"' He paced across to the small chest of drawers and back again. 'At least you could have been candid with me about your reasons for calling our wedding off.'

'I have been,' Ashleigh said. 'It would be dishonest of me to marry you feeling the way I do at the moment.'

'Dishonest!' Jonathan exclaimed. 'That's the most honest word you've used to date!'

'Oh, what's the use?' Ashleigh knew she was on the verge of tears. 'Jon, I'm tired and I'm upset and I think it would be best if we call this evening quits. Maybe in the morning we'll be able to behave like rational adults.'

'That will be too late, Ashleigh. I'm leaving in the morning and I want this settled tonight.'

'Jon, please, no ultimatums. I've had just about enough, more than I can stand.' She pulled her engagement ring from her finger and walking across the room she held it out to him. 'Please believe me, I am sorry. I think we . . . we made the mistake of thinking the habit we drifted into was reason enough for marriage, and that could never be enough.'

He looked down at the ring before slowly pocketing it. 'If you decide not to come with me tomorrow, Ashleigh, I won't take you back when you come to your senses,' he said flatly.

Ashleigh stood looking at him. 'I'd already decided not to come back with you,' she told him quietly. 'Now I'd like to go home.'

He made no move to step aside but remained where he was, blocking her exit to the door. 'You took my ring off so easily.' His face had grown flushed and his eyes were coldly angry. 'Are you planning on slipping on another with as little ease, I wonder?'

'Let me pass, Jonathan. I'll ring for a taxi.' She went to step around him, but his hands shot out and fastened on her arms with uncharacteristic forcefulness. 'Answer me, Ashleigh!'

'I told you before, you're mistaken.'

'Am I?'

Ashleigh's anger erupted. 'For heaven's sake, Jonathan, I'm beginning to believe that's what you want me to say, and I can't understand why, what possible reason you could have for it.'

'Don't try to put me off. I saw the way you kept giving Patrick those coquettish little looks all evening. You were flirting with him right under my nose. How do you think that made me look?' His hands tightened on her arms, his fingers biting into the soft flesh.

'Jon, let me go! You're hurting me.'

'And he couldn't keep his eyes off you either.' He ignored her pleas. 'I should have knocked him down!'

'Jon, don't . . .'

'I think you'd better tell me exactly what went on while you were marooned on that island. If you ever were marooned.' His lip curled derogatorily.

'I'm not . . . I refuse to talk to you while you're in this mood,' said Ashleigh with as much conviction as she could scrape together. 'Please let me go!'

'It was all so romantic, wasn't it, Ashleigh?' He continued as though she hadn't spoken. 'The deserted beach, the two of you alone. You can't tell me he didn't make a pass at you. He's the type who wouldn't let a chance like that pass him by. It's written all over him.'

Ashleigh's pale face flushed red and her lips began to tremble, knowing she couldn't deny that particular accusation.

He gave a harsh laugh at her hesitation. 'The guilt's all over your face, my dear. You've made a fool out of me, Ashleigh, and I don't like it. All these years I've been under the misapprehension that you preferred a gentlemanly approach while you've been passing out your favours behind my back. How many others have there been before him?'

'That's despicable!' Ashleigh burst out. 'How can you even suggest that?'

'Are you denying it?' he asked clippedly.

'Of course I'm denying it. But you're just going to have to take my word for it.'

A flicker of indecision passed over his face and his hold on her relaxed slightly, but when she went to brush past him he caught her to him, his arms sliding around her.

'Not so fast, Ashleigh. I'm beginning to think it's time I changed my tactics. I think I deserve something for keeping my hands off all this time.'

Ashleigh stared up at him in horror, her head moving slowly from side to side in silent negation as his lips came down to crush hers. She pushed ineffectually against him, but he held her fast, the pres-

sure of his lips bruising. When he raised his head he
was breathing heavily, but he released her, allowing
her to step away from him.

'How could you, Jon?' Her voice was almost a whisper as she forced the words out through tight lips, her
fingers moving to cover them as she fought an urge to
scrub the imprint of his punishing kiss from her
mouth.

'Don't try to feign innocence,' he said brutally. 'Just
be thankful I'm settling for a kiss. If I didn't think I'd
be lowering myself to joining the long line I'd push for
a more intimate reward!'

Her hand snaked out, catching him across his cheek,
leaving a dull red stain. He glared back at her with
cold disdain as his hand massaged his jaw. Their eyes
held for some seconds before he turned his back on
her, leaving her way to the door clear.

'Just get out, Ashleigh. I can't bear to look at you,'
he said frigidly. 'And Ashleigh,' his words caused her
to falter, 'don't think this leaves me high and dry, because it doesn't. I've better fish to fry!'

Wrenching open the door, Ashleigh almost ran down
the corridor, tears spilling on to her cheeks before she
had taken half a dozen steps. Her face burned as
Jonathan's words came back to her and she crossed the
lighted foyer of the hotel with head downcast, set upon
reaching the street and the relative obscurity of the
night. She knew she'd have to find a telephone to call
a taxi, but she needed a few moments to get herself
together before she returned to face Gemma.

Halfway down the few steps to the footpath she
cannoned into a rock-solid body, and as firm hands
came out to steady her she looked up through a haze of
tears into the familiar hard planes of Mitch's face. She

tried to dash her tears away before he could see them, but he caught her hands, turning her slightly sideways so that the light could fall directly on her face.

'Ashleigh? What's the matter? Didn't he take it the way you expected?' he asked cruelly, and a fresh wave of tears cascaded down her cheeks.

His jaw tensed and after a moment he took a deep breath. 'What happened?' he asked with tempered quietness, his change of tone almost her complete undoing.

'Nothing. I . . . we just had words and . . .' her voice caught on a sob.

His eyes moved over her, settling on her trembling lips, his sharp assessment not missing the angry red marks on her arms where Jonathan had held her. 'Where is he?' he asked with frightening coldness.

'He . . . why?' Ashleigh blinked the wetness from her eyes and caught her breath at the steel flash of aggression in Mitch's expression. 'No, Mitch, please! I just want to forget it. I . . . If you could call me a taxi I'll go back to the flat.' Her hand on his arm stayed his progress up the stairs.

For what seemed like a millennium to Ashleigh he stood poised there before he turned away and taking her arm he led her a short distance up the street to his Range Rover. Putting her inside, he walked around and slid behind the wheel, flicking the engine to life and pulling away from the kerb.

'You needn't have taken me home. I . . . If you were going somewhere . . .' Her voice faded, but he made no comment. 'Mitch?'

He shot her one quick glance, but the confines of the cabin were too shadowed for her to gauge his expression.

'I wasn't going anywhere in particular,' he said at last, 'Except for a stiff drink. Or maybe two,' he added flatly.

A tense silence fell again.

'Where's Megan?' Ashleigh asked before she could stop herself.

'In her flat. In bed, I presume,' he replied shortly.

'Oh.'

She heard him swear under his breath before he swung the Range Rover off the road down a narrow track and pulled to a halt on a grassy verge overlooking the beach and the dark water. When he moved she jumped and her eyes turned uneasily towards him, but he was only reaching for a cigarette, his lighter flaring as he lit up, momentarily illuminating the rugged familiarity of his tanned face. 'Mitch, I'm rather tired and I'd like to go home,' Ashleigh said shakily, her heart beating wildly at his nearness.

'What did good old Jonathan do that upset you so much?' he asked. 'Didn't he feel inclined to give you up as easily as you thought he would?'

Ashleigh could almost laugh at that, but the laughter caught in her throat and became a sob that she had to swallow convulsively before she spoke. 'I don't really care to talk about it. It's between Jonathan and me.'

'And none of my business,' he finished, and gave a humourless exclamation. 'That's quite a laugh!' He turned to face her, twisting slightly in the seat so that his knees were mere inches from hers. 'Haven't you cottoned on yet, Ashleigh? You are my business, it seems, whether I like it or not.'

'Mitch, I don't feel like any more tonight. Please take me back to Gemma's.' Ashleigh ran a shaky hand over her eyes and he reached across and took hold of it, clasping it tightly, his fingers feeling for her engagement ring.

Raising her ringless hand to his lips, he kissed her palm. 'Don't lose any sleep over him, Ashleigh. He wouldn't have made you happy, not in a million years.'

Pulling her hand out of his grasp, Ashleigh turned to gaze out at the water. If his lips touched her at that moment she would have completely broken down, and she fought to regain her composure. 'Do you think that makes it any easier? For me or for Jonathan?'

His arm slid around the back of her, fingers playing over the nape of her neck as he levered himself closer along the seat until his warm leg touched hers and she swallowed quickly, turning to face him. 'Forget him, Ashleigh. Now's what counts,' he said huskily. 'You and me.' His lips moved gently over hers and she felt the rising sensations begin to wash over her, blotting out everything—Jonathan, the bitterness—leaving only Mitch's hardness pressed against her, his hands caressing, his lips softly arousing, gently persuasive, gradually growing more fervent in their demand.

'Ashleigh, what you do to me!' His voice came raggedly from deep in his chest as his lips nuzzled her earlobe, sending sensual signals along her nerve ends. 'You tear me apart so badly I can't think straight. Much more of this and I'll end up a raving lunatic!' His leg moved over hers insistently, arousing her so that she arched against him, her body trembling with desire. 'God, Ash, I want you!' he breathed huskily.

She wanted him, too—how she wanted him, needed him, loved him. Loved him so much that it was a pain deep within her, far deeper than a physical need for fulfilment. 'Oh, Mitch,' she muttered brokenly into the thick fairness of his hair as his lips found the pulse at the base of her throat. 'I love you.' The words were murmured softly.

'Come back to the flat with me,' he said urgently.

'But Gemma . . .'

'You can ring her in the morning,' his lips nibbled on her bottom lip, 'let her know you're moving in with me.' His kiss claimed her with such devastating demand that she almost drowned in the sensation, and only when he raised his head did the full impact of his words hit her with agonising suddenness.

'Mitch?' Her eyes strained to focus on the shadowy planes of his face. 'What . . . what do you mean?' she asked huskily.

'I mean you're moving into the flat with me. We can have a good thing going, Ash. We're tuned in the same key to the same melody, you can't deny that.' He ran one finger slowly down her cheek, across to her lips, feeling their trembling.

Her body remained stiffly where it was, her tension soon communicating itself to him, and he sat a little away from her.

'All right,' he said flatly, 'don't tell me, let me guess. You're still for the white lace.'

'There doesn't have to be white lace, Mitch,' she replied quietly. 'But there has to be more of a commitment than you're offering.'

'I see.' He ran his hands over his knees and slid back behind the wheel.

'Do you, Mitch? I don't somehow think you do. I can't be just a one-night, one-week, maybe one-month stand. It's not enough.'

'Who said anything about time?' he said sharply. 'It's each day that matters. Now. One day at a time.'

She could feel his eyes on her and she longed desperately to throw herself back into his arms, take what he offered for as long as he offered it, but she couldn't do it. She knew she didn't have the strength to live on that particular type of tightrope. She loved him too much. 'I'm sorry, Mitch,' she whispered before her throat closed on a sob.

He sat there for immeasurable seconds before he started the Range Rover and reversed back onto the road with sharp precise movements and they were at Gemma's flat in a matter of minutes.

'Thank you,' Ashleigh got out, 'for bringing me home.' And she had the door open before he spoke.

'When are you going back to Brisbane?'

'I don't know. I ... it's less than a week to Christmas, so I may spend Christmas with Gemma and ... and go home for New Year.'

'Then I guess I won't see you before you leave,' he said expressionlessly. 'I'm flying north tomorrow, taking Megan back. And I suppose I'll spend Christmas with my family.'

Ashleigh's heart contracted painfully.

'Goodbye, Ashleigh,' he said with finality, not looking at her.

'Mitch, I ... Goodbye.' She jumped down from the Range Rover and walked quickly to the flat, letting herself inside as quietly as possible, grateful that Gemma hadn't waited up for her, and it wasn't until she closed the door of her room that the tears fell.

How she made it through the next few days Ashleigh would never be able to say. Perhaps she used Mitch's concept of taking a day at a time, but she knew that somewhere deep inside her part of her had died, ceased to function, perhaps never would again.

She wrote a short letter to her mother giving her the barest details of the situation, only explaining that she couldn't marry Jonathan because she had discovered they didn't love each other enough. She received a long letter from her mother by return mail, full of disjointed questions, with a short postscript from her father saying they respected her decision and agreeing that a few more days with Gemma was a good idea. Jonathan didn't contact her before he left for Brisbane.

With Gemma back at work Ashleigh had the days to herself, and she spent them sunbathing by the pool at the back of the flats, carefully keeping her mind lazily blank, forbidding any thought of Mitch to materialise from her shrouded memory.

With a shock she realised today was Christmas Eve, and she sighed softly. She should get up and go for an invigorating swim or go inside and sort out her Christmas gifts, but it was all too much of an effort. She preferred to simply drift in this painless, numbing void. Closing her eyes, she settled herself more comfortably on the patio chair.

Ashleigh sensed rather than heard the soft footfalls on the springy grass and she drowsily turned her head, expecting to see one of the other tenants or perhaps Gemma home for lunch. His shadow slid over her as he stood towering beside her for a moment before he lowered himself on to the grass near her lounger.

As she stared back at him, watching as he absently pulled a blade of grass and put it between his teeth, the heavy deadness inside her tingled to life and she closed her eyes, wanting to blank him out again, steel herself against any more hurt that he might mete out to her. But her mental picture of him swam in the darkness behind her lids, refusing to fade.

In those first few moments she had seen and absorbed every part of him, from the tip of his fair hair to his sneaker-clad feet. She had taken in the dark thick denim of his jeans, the whiteness of his light shirt that moulded the contours of a body the feel of which she could never erase from her mind, the bright blueness of his eyes as they made a quick sweep of her supine bikini-clad body.

'When did you get back?' she asked at last, her voice a little high and shaky.

'About fifteen minutes ago.' He spoke for the first time, his voice that same deep huskiness. 'I went straight to the bank to check with Gemma, and she said you'd most probably be here by the pool.'

'Oh!'

'Aren't you going to ask me why I'm here?' he continued after a pause.

'Yes.' Ashleigh was having trouble summoning enough breath to form words.

'You sound terribly enthusiastic,' he said with a harshness that was mostly self-derisive. 'I'm overwhelmed.'

'Mitch, please!' she beseeched softly. 'Don't . . .' She took a steady breath. 'Since you went away I've managed to regain my equilibrium to some extent, but it's still wavering on fragile ground and I don't want you to—well, I don't think I can take much more upset,' she finished quickly, her hands grasped together in her lap to still their trembling.

He took a slow breath, his eyes fixed on the blade of grass he twirled slowly between his fingers. 'I'm sorry, Ashleigh—belatedly, I know, but nevertheless I am sorry I hurt you. If it's any consolation, I hurt myself more.'

Ashleigh watched the lines of his profile, noticing the fatigue in his face for the first time.

'I discovered that fact in these past few days. In hurting you I tortured myself, and that's a first for me, something I've never experienced before. As I told you on more than one occasion,' he grimaced, 'I was only interested in the moment, and when a girl began to hear the Wedding March I bowed out very neatly. With most of them it was an amicable parting—they knew the score. I'm not proud of it, but it's got to be said. I want to be honest with you.'

'Mitch, there's really no need to . . .' Ashleigh began.

'*I* need to, Ash.' He looked across at her. 'When I flew home to the Tableland I went for a specific reason—to get you completely and irrevocably out of my system. Simple.' He gave a soft laugh. 'It didn't quite work out that way, somehow. Not only did I fail to wipe you out of my mind but I couldn't get you out of my heart. Every day away from you became more of an agony. I couldn't eat, couldn't sleep. I worked myself into the ground.'

He picked up one of her hands and gently rubbed it with his thumb. 'Then this morning I was riding up at the top end of the farm feeling like death when it suddenly hit me like a thunderbolt.' His eyes held hers. 'I didn't want you out of my life—not now, not ever. I wanted you for my life, Ash—marriage, kids, the whole bit. All the things I've decried so vehemently in the past. They never meant anything to me before because I hadn't met you. Although I didn't recognise it I know now I've been waiting for you.'

He raised her hand to his lips and kissed her palm,

and Ashleigh felt herself come alive. She ran her hand along his jaw and let her fingers slide into his hair, tears spilling on to her cheeks. In one sure movement he pulled her out of the chair and on to his lap, his lips resting against her temple, holding her close.

'Did you mean it?' he asked quietly. 'What you said in the car the other night?'

'Did I mean what?' Ashleigh stammered.

'That you loved me.' He leant back so that he could look into her face and when she nodded he crushed her to him. 'Thank God for that,' he laughed huskily. 'I've been clinging to that like a security blanket!' Mitch kissed her soundly and then raised his head. 'I love you, too, Ashleigh,' he said seriously. 'I think I knew it all along, but in my self-assured arrogance I didn't want to admit it, didn't want to lose face. The great Mitch Patrick, advocate of free love, etc., etc., not only losing face but caught out with pie all over it!'

'Mitch, I never meant to . . .' Ashleigh stopped when he put one finger on her lips.

'I know you didn't. But you did. I was yours from the moment I first saw you at the airport. Why do you think I was so offhand with you? Because I had a pretty fair premonition even then that I'd never be the same again. Oh, I thought I could handle it, especially when you gave me the cold shoulder. I was going to handle it all right, have you eating out of my hand in no time. I knew I was a mild success with the ladies. My physical attraction, as you called it,' he pulled a face at her and Ashleigh flushed. 'The fact that you were flashing me the red light only made you more of a challenge.' His smile faded. 'Then I walked into Gemma's flat with Joel and you were standing there smiling at everyone. Everyone but me, that was. I felt as if I'd been hit right between the eyes with a piece of three by two.'

'That bad?' Ashleigh teased him, the dimples appearing in her cheeks and he traced one indentation with his fingers.

'That bad,' he said with conviction. 'Not that I gave in to it. But I hadn't reckoned on you, Ashleigh. I played all the wrong cards even though I'd been dealt the best hand. The very best hand,' he repeated softly, his lips finding hers, and they clung together until they were both breathless.

'I love you, Ash, and I want you to come and live with me, all signed, sealed, and for life,' he said huskily.

Tears caught in Ashleigh's throat and she could only nod her head, her lips finding the strong column of his throat as she moulded herself against him. His lips claimed hers again, his kiss hardening, firm hands sliding sensuously around her bare midriff, until he groaned softly and held her from him. Looking around at the open pool area and their lack of privacy, he grinned lopsidedly.

'I wish we were back on the island,' he said ruefully, and Ashleigh laughed breathlessly.

'We could always spend our honeymoon there.'

'Now there's a thought,' he chuckled. 'A very historic place, that island. Or at least it will be for our grandchildren, especially when I tell them that was where their grandmother tried to seduce me.'

Ashleigh blushed and then looked indignant. 'You would tell them that, too, wouldn't you?'

Mitch nodded, teasingly. 'Oh, Ashleigh, I want to take you inside, but if I do . . .' His eyes blazed. 'I feel I should warn you, my love, that I'm going to need a few cheap avaricious thrills every once in a while. That was what you called it that morning on the island, wasn't it? Cheap avaricious thrills?'

'I did say that, didn't I?' She grinned sheepishly and Mitch nodded. 'It wasn't very nice of me after . . . after what happened the night before.'

'Most definitely wasn't,' he agreed, and pulled her to him. 'Damn! This place is far too public for what I have in mind,' he said against her earlobe, and stood up, lifting her with him. 'When it comes to cheap avaricious thrills I want you all to myself.' And with that he swung her into his arms and strode purposefully towards the flat.

Harlequin® Plus
PORTENTS OF LOVE

Hoping for a chance at love?

Here are seven love superstitions that may foretell your love life:

Put a four-leaf clover over your front door; the first man to enter will be the man you marry.

Cut an apple in two and repeat aloud the name of the one you love. If the apple contains twelve seeds, you will marry him.

When you have the hiccups, think of the one you love. If your hiccups stop right away, he returns your love. If they continue, you should probably forget him.

You can have any man you want by walking nine ties of a railroad track without stepping off the ties.

Trim your fingernails every Sunday for nine weeks and you can have the man of your choosing.

If you feel a sneeze coming on, turn your thoughts to your sweetheart and press your finger to your upper lip. If you don't sneeze, your sweetheart loves you.

The first man whose hand you shake after rubbing your hands in sweet fern is your true love.

The bestselling epic saga of the Irish!
An intriguing and passionate story that spans 400 years.

FIRST...
The Defiant

Lady Elizabeth Hatton, highborn Englishwoman, was not above using her position to get what she wanted ...and more than anything in the world she wanted Rory O'Donnell, the fiery Irish rebel. But it was an alliance that promised only ruin....

THEN...
The Survivors

Against a turbulent background of political intrigue and royal corruption, the determined, passionate Shanna O'Hara searched for peace in her beloved but troubled Ireland. Meanwhile in England, hot-tempered Brenna Coke fought against a loveless marriage....

649 Ontario Street
Stratford, Ontario N5A 6W2

P.O. Box 22188
Tempe, AZ 85282

Readers rave about Harlequin romance fiction...

"I absolutely adore Harlequin romances! They are fun and relaxing to read, and each book provides a wonderful escape."
—N.E.,* Pacific Palisades, California

"Harlequin is the best in romantic reading."
—K.G., Philadelphia, Pennsylvania

"Harlequin romances give me a whole new outlook on life."
—S.P., Mecosta, Michigan

"My praise for the warmth and adventure your books bring into my life."
—D.F., Hicksville, New York

*Names available on request.